Agatha Christie®

The Rule of Three

Agatha Christie

A SAMUEL FRENCH ACTING EDITION

FOUNDED 1830

SAMUELFRENCH.COM
SAMUELFRENCH-LONDON.CO.UK

FOR PRODUCTION ENQUIRIES

UNITED STATES AND CANADA
Info@SamuelFrench.com
1-866-598-8449

UNITED KINGDOM AND EUROPE
Plays@SamuelFrench-London.co.uk
020-7255-4302

Each title is subject to availability from Samuel French, depending upon country of performance. Please be aware that *THE MOUSETRAP* may not be licensed by Samuel French in your territory. Professional and amateur producers should contact the nearest Samuel French office or licensing partner to verify availability.

MUSIC USE NOTE

IMPORTANT BILLING AND CREDIT REQUIREMENTS

CONTENTS

Afternoon at
the Seaside

AFTERNOON AT THE SEASIDE was first presented by Peter Saundersat the Duchess Theatre, London, on 20th December 1962. The performance was directed by Hubert Gregg, with sets by Peter Rice. The cast was as follows:

BOB WHEELER	David Langton
NOREEN SOMERS	Betty McDowall
ARTHUR SOMERS	Michael Beint
GEORGE CRUM	Robert Raglan
MRS. CRUM	Mabelle George
A MOTHER	Vera Cook
A YOUNG MAN	John Quayle
BEACH ATTENDANT	John Abineri
MRS GUNNER (MOM)	Margot Boyd
PERCY GUNNER	Raymond Bowers
THE BEAUTY	Mercy Haystead
INSPECTOR FOLEY	Robin May

CHARACTERS

BOB WHEELER
NOREEN SOMERSl
ARTHUR SOMERS
GEORGE CRUMn
MRS. CRUM
A MOTHER
A YOUNG MAN
BEACH ATTENDANT
MRS GUNNER (MOM)
PERCY GUNNER
THE BEAUTY
INSPECTOR FOLEY

SETTING

The beach at Little-Slippyng-on-Sea, a summer afternoon

(Scene: The beach. A summer afternoon.)

(Three bathing huts face the audience on a rostrum. That on the right is labelled Bide-a-Wee. The middle one is Mon Desir, that on the left Ben Nevis. In front of the huts is an asphalted walk reached by a ramp and three steps up left. Extreme right is a beach telescope for viewing the bay. In the foreground, below the rostrum and reached by short sets of steps before each hut, is an assortment of beach litter, banana skins, empty cigarette cartons, odd bathing towels, a shrimping net and an abandoned sand castle. To left of these is a deck chair.)

(As the curtain rises, or just before, voices are heard singing "I do like to be beside the seaside," rather out of tune.)

(When the curtain rises, the lights fade up from a black-out. The doors of Mon Desir and Ben Nevis are closed, but Bide-a-Wee is open and shows itself full of equipment, cups, etc., on hooks, coats, folded table and chairs – in fact quite a home from home. In front of it, in two canvas upright chairs, sit MR and MRS. CRUM. GEORGE sits right and MRS. CRUM, left. MR. CRUM is elderly, fat and outwardly submissive to MRS. CRUM, who is fifty-two, loquacious and generally censorious. She is knitting and he is trying to read the local afternoon paper. On the beach left, roughly in front of Ben Nevis, MRS SOMERS and BOB WHEELER are sprawling on the sands in bathing dresses. NOREEN SOMERS is a good-looking, rather blowsy woman of thirty-odd with enormous vivacity. BOB WHEELER is about the same age, a terrific wag, and sure to be the life and soul of any gathering. MR. SOMERS is sitting in a deck-chair left, wearing an overcoat and scarf, with a heavy stick propped by him. He looks grey and tired. A heap of clothes

*lies by these three where they have undressed on the b
each – grey flannel trousers, cotton frock, slip, etc.
NOREEN SOMERS is adorning a large and handsome
sand castle with cockle shells. Off left a small child
is bawling at the top of his voice. Dogs are barking
intermittently.)*

BOB. *(removing a bucket from the top of the sand castle)* There
you are.

NOREEN. There's a clever boy.

BOB. A fairy castle for the girl of my dreams.

NOREEN. Better not let Arthur hear you.

BOB. He's asleep.

NOREEN. Just as well.

BOB. Girl of my dreams, I love you. *(He takes a sweet from a
chocolate box and eats it.)* Honest, I do.

NOREEN. Hey, that was my last soft centre. *(She throws the
box on the sand right of* **BOB***.)*

BOB. *(taking the box and throwing it towards a little bin right)*
Ay, ay. Keep Britain tidy.

*(A jet aeroplane is heard flying overhead, followed by the
barking of a dog.)*

NOREEN. Any more shells?

BOB. *(picking up a shell from the sand)* Here you are, Noreen.
Here's a beauty.

*(A **MOTHER** enters right, crossing to left.)*

MOTHER. Ernie! Ernie! Stop it, I say! *(to* **BOB***, at his right)*
No, not you. I'm talking to my son. Leave that dog
alone – it'll bite you! *(She stands by the exit down left.)*

NOREEN. Ta, ever so.

*(A beach ball bounces on from left, followed by a **YOUNG
MAN**, who clambers over the people on the sand for the
ball, and exits left.)*

YOUNG MAN. Sorry. Sorry. Sorry.

MOTHER. Ernie!

BOB. Never a dull moment at the seaside, that's what I always say.

MOTHER. Why don't you go and have a paddle? Look at Bert, he's paddling. Why don't you go and paddle too?

CHILD. *(off)* Don't wanna paddle – wah!

MOTHER. Bring you to the seaside I do to enjoy yourself, and what happens? You bawl your head off.

CHILD. *(off)* Don't want to – wah!

MOTHER. Well, I'm going to enjoy myself if it's the last thing I do.

CHILD. *(off) Waaah!*

MOTHER. Oh, shut up! *(She crosses right, above* **BOB**.*)*

BOB. Kids, eh?

MOTHER. *(turning and looking at* **BOB***)* What!!! *(She turns away.)*

(The **MOTHER** *exits right.)*

NOREEN. First time I went to the seaside I yelled my head off. Said the sea was wet and the sand was dirty You never enjoy a thing first time you do it.

BOB. That's right. Goes for other things than the seaside, eh, Norrie?

NOREEN. Now, Bob, steady! You'll shock Arthur here.

BOB. *(looking at* **MR. SOMERS**, *who does not react at all)* Couldn't shock old Arthur. Nothing shocks Arthur, does it, Artie?

*(***MR. SOMERS** *merely smiles in a tired way.)*

NOREEN. *(kneeling and taking a bathing-cap from her beach-bag)* Oh, well, I'm going in for my second dip. Come on, Bob.

BOB. Too bloomin' cold.

NOREEN. Slacker!

BOB. Women don't feel the cold. *(eyeing her)* Too well covered. *(He smacks her bottom.)*

NOREEN. You give over. *(She rises.)* I'll race you to the jetty.

BOB. *(rising to the ramp left)* Right. On your marks. Get set. *(He runs off down left.)*

NOREEN. *(following him)* Hey, you cheated!

*(**BOB** and **NOREEN** exit down left. **MR. SOMERS** rises, puts down his newspaper, picks up his stick, and goes up the ramp and steps to exit off up left.)*

MRS. CRUM. *(watching in disapproval)* I must say, George, that Little-Slippyng isn't what it was.

GEORGE. Little-Slippyng slipping, eh?

MRS. CRUM. *Quite* a different class of people nowadays. I've a good mind not to come here next year.

GEORGE. Ar…

MRS. CRUM. Talking and screaming and making those very doubtful jokes! Just as though they were alone on the beach.

GEORGE. Needn't listen, my dear.

MRS. CRUM. What did you say?

GEORGE. Said you needn't listen.

MRS. CRUM. *(sharply)* Don't talk nonsense, George.

GEORGE. No, my dear.

MRS. CRUM. And that one with all the jokes isn't even her husband. It's the other one she's married to.

GEORGE. How do you know?

*(The beach ball comes in from left right on to the rostrum. The **YOUNG MAN** follows it.)*

MRS. CRUM. Well, really!

YOUNG MAN. Sorry. *(He retrieves the ball.)*

*(The **YOUNG MAN** exits left.)*

MRS. CRUM. Mothers who can't control their children! Young men and girls with next to nothing on, kicking balls all over the place. No consideration for those who want to sit peacefully and enjoy themselves.

GEORGE. Only young once.

MRS. CRUM. That's a foolish thing to say – very foolish indeed.

GEORGE. Yes, dear.

MRS. CRUM. We didn't behave like that when we were young. *(She leans over to take wool from the bag at the side of her chair.)* And in my mother's day, men and girls bathed from different beaches even.

GEORGE. That can't have been much fun.

MRS. CRUM. *(sitting up)* What did you say?

GEORGE. Nothing, dear, Nothing at all. Seems there was a burglary here last night.

MRS. CRUM. At Little-Slippyng?

GEORGE. Yes. Lady Beckman.

MRS. CRUM. What – the Lady Beckman that has all those mink coats and the lovely Rollses? Is she down here?

GEORGE. Esplanade Hotel.

MRS. CRUM. What was taken – a mink coat?

GEORGE. No. Emerald necklace.

MRS. CRUM. An...? *(sitting up)* Oh? *(She resumes knitting.)* Oh, well, I dare say she's got half a dozen of those, too. I wonder she even noticed it was gone!

(MR. SOMERS enters down the ramp left, moves to his deck-chair, and sits.)

GEORGE. Cat burglar, they think. Got in through the bathroom window after crawling up a drainpipe while the dancing was going on in the evening.

MRS. CRUM. Serves her right!

(The BEACH ATTENDANT, a very old man in uniform, with rheumy eyes and a red nose, enters down left to above MR. SOMERS.)

BEACH ATTENDANT. Fourpence, please. *(He takes off his cap, wipes his head, and replaces the cap.)*

(MR. SOMERS is busy reading a magazine.)

Fourpence for the chair.

MR. SOMERS. Oh! *(He finds a florin.)*

(The **BEACH ATTENDANT** *punches a ticket, gives it to* **MR. SOMERS,** *takes the florin from him.)*

Nice afternoon – quite warm.

(The **BEACH ATTENDANT** *gets change from his money bag and counts it into* **MR. SOMERS**'s *hand.)*

BEACH ATTENDANT. Sixpence, shillin', two shillin's. *(gloomily)* Too nice an afternoon makes a lot of trouble. You should see the parking lot! Regular mix up! Some of them cars won't get out for hours.

MR. SOMERS. Isn't there someone to control it?

BEACH ATTENDANT. Ah – old Joe – but it's more than one man can manage. Cars coming in in a stream ever since lunch-time and parking themselves where they please. Ah, I remember this place when there wasn't more than a couple of dozen on the beach – all residents they were – quiet and well be'aved... *(He breaks off, looking off left, and suddenly yells.)* Hey – you! Stop throwin' stones, you'll 'it someone! *(to* **MR. SOMERS** *and the world)* Boys! Always up to something. *(He looks out front, looks at his watch, and blows his whistle.)* Hey, you – float number twelve – you've 'ad your half-hour! Come in! *(He pauses.)* Eh?

(The **BEACH ATTENDANT** *exits right, blowing his whistle.)*

MRS. CRUM. *(her hands to her ears)* That whistle.

(The beach ball bounds on from left and hits **GEORGE.** *The* **YOUNG MAN** *enters from left, even more out of breath.)*

YOUNG MAN. Sorry! *(He retrieves the ball and throws it off left.)*

(There is an agonized protest from **MRS GUNNER** *["*MOM*"] off left.)*

Sorry.

(The **YOUNG MAN** *exits left.* **MOM** *enters left as the* **YOUNG MAN** *exits, brushing sand off herself. She is a*

possessive old battle-axe. **PERCY**, *her son, follows her on.*
He is a nice but sad **YOUNG MAN**.)

MOM. Well, I don't know what the young are coming to!
(She goes up the ramp to right of Ben Nevis.)

(**PERCY** *follows* **MOM** *to her left.*)

I really don't! Sand all over me! Now, Percy, open the
house. *(She gives the key to* **PERCY**.)

(**PERCY** *opens the hut, takes out* **MOM**'s *chair and puts
it right of the hut.*)

MRS. CRUM. Good afternoon, Mrs Gunner.

MOM. Good afternoon, Mrs. Crum. Good afternoon,
Mr Crum.

(**GEORGE** *raises his hat, still reading.*)

PERCY. *(placing the chair facing front)* Here you are, Mom.
Which way would you like it?

MOM. That's very nice, thank you, dear. *(She sits.)*

(**PERCY** *brings out his chair, and puts it left of the hut.*)

No, I think I'll have it a bit more round. *(She rises.)*

(**PERCY** *moves her chair to face farther left.* **MOM** *sits.*
PERCY *sits.*)

And my knitting.

(**PERCY** *rises, brings her knitting and a towel out of the
hut, places the towel on his chair and the knitting on*
MOM's *left.*)

That's it. On the other side.

(**PERCY** *moves the knitting to right of* **MOM**. **MOM** *puts
her bag on her left.* **PERCY** *gives her the key, and sits.*
Quite a business is made of it all.)

(fondly) He's such a good son to me.

(**PERCY** *is embarrassed.*)

Not that I want to keep him always waiting on me. "You
must leave me and go and enjoy yourself," I say. We old
women must expect to sit back and take second place.

He wouldn't go to the pictures last night because he thought I had a bit of a headache.

MRS. CRUM. That's nice. That's very nice. That's what I like to hear.

GEORGE. *Did* you have a headache?

MOM. *(with dignity)* It passed off. *(She sorts out her knitting.)*

GEORGE. I'll bet it did. It was never damned well there in the first place.

*(**MRS. CRUM** glares at **GEORGE**, who stops.)*

YOUNG MAN. *(off left)* Per-cie. Per-cie – come on – we've been waiting for you.

PERCY. *(rising to the edge of the rostrum)* Hy!

MOM. Who's that, dear? *(shading her eyes)* I can't see.

PERCY. It's Edie and Tom.

MOM. Edie – is that the red-haired girl who wanted you to go on the charabanc trip?

PERCY. *(moving down the ramp)* That's right – that's Edie. They've got a boat.

*(**PERCY** goes off down left.)*

MOM. I don't think there's time for that today, Percy.

*(**PERCY** re-enters, standing down left.)*

I might want you to get me another skein of wool before the shops shut.

PERCY. *(standing down left)* Well – I kind of promised…

MOM. *(martyred) Of course* go if you want to, dear. I never want to stand in the way of you enjoying yourself. I know only too well what a trouble we old people are.

PERCY. *(crossing up to **MOM**)* Oh, look here, Mom…

MOM. I dare say I can manage to get to the shops myself – if it's not too hot. It's just I feel my heart a little.

*(**GEORGE** blows his nose.)*

PERCY. No, no. I'll get your wool. I don't know that I want to go out in the boat.

MOM. You don't really like going on the sea, do you, dear? Even as a little boy, you weren't a good sailor.

PERCY. It's calm enough today. I'd better tell them.

(**PERCY** *exits down left, dejected.*)

MOM. (*with satisfaction*) I knew he didn't really want to go. Percy's so good-natured – and these girls just badger a man so that he doesn't like to refuse. That Edie now – quite the wrong type for Percy.

MRS. CRUM. It's lucky he's got you to look after him.

MOM. Yes. Now if a really nice girl came along, I'd be only too pleased for Percy to be friendly with her.

GEORGE. Would you?

MOM. (*with a delightful laugh*) Oh, yes. Nothing of the grudging mother about *me*. Some mothers can't bear their sons to go about with other people. I'm only too pleased. I wish Percy would do it more. But he's so devoted to me that I really can't persuade him to leave me. "You're better company than any girl, Mom," he says. Ridiculous, isn't it?

GEORGE. Yes.

MRS. CRUM. (*glaring at* **GEORGE,** *and smiling at* **MOM**) Ah, there's a lot of truth in the old saying that a boy's best friend is his mother.

(*The* **BEAUTY** *steps out of Mon Desir. She is a true pin-up girl. She is wearing a daring bikini and a good deal of make-up, and looks very exotic and slightly foreign. She has an elaborate bag and a vanity case. Possibly a beach wrap with "Je t'aime, I love you, Ich liebe dich," etc., patterned all over it. She turns to close the door.* **MRS. CRUM** *and* **MOM** *look her up and down.*)

BEAUTY. (*after standing for a moment, seemingly unconscious of all around her, but with a suggestion of a model posing*) Mesdames, Messieurs, good afternoon! (*She goes down on to the sand and sits centre.*)

(**MRS. CRUM** *and* **MOM** *look at each other, then at* **BEAUTY.**)

MOM. French!!

*(They knit. **GEORGE** leans forward to stare goggle-eyed.
MR. SOMERS also cranes his neck round and stares.
BEAUTY takes out a cigarette-case from her bag, and a
lighter which will not light. **GEORGE** and **MR. SOMERS**
rise to her assistance. **GEORGE** lights her cigarette. The
men exchange a look.)*

BEAUTY. *(to **GEORGE**; with a breath-taking smile and a slight
accent)* Oh, thank you. You are so kind.

GEORGE. *(incoherent)* Not at all – not at all – pleasure.

*(The men start to return. **BEAUTY** drops her lighter.
MR SOMERS reaches it and hands it to her. **GEORGE**
looks on.)*

BEAUTY. *(transferring her smile to **MR. SOMERS**)* Oh, but I am
stupid. Thank you very much.

MR. SOMERS. Delighted – no trouble…

(The men exchange a look, and return to their seats.)

MRS. CRUM. *(coldly)* What's on at the Pier Pavilion tonight,
George?

GEORGE. *(still goggling at **BEAUTY**)* Yes?

MRS. CRUM. George, didn't you hear me?

GEORGE. Eh? What?

MRS. CRUM. I – said – what's – on – at – the – Pavilion?

GEORGE. *(flustered, looking at the paper)* Oh – yes – *The
Woman Tempted Me.* (He looks at **BEAUTY**, at **MRS. CRUM**,
then away.)

*(There is a slight pause, then **BEAUTY** rises, discards her
wrap, and places it and the beach bag on the rostrum.
The ball bounces on. **BEAUTY** fends it off. The **YOUNG
MAN** enters, sees her and begins to dither. **BEAUTY**
laughs.)*

YOUNG MAN. *(left of **BEAUTY**)* I'm ever so sorry. I am – reely.

BEAUTY. But it is quite all right. It did not hurt me.

YOUNG MAN. Oh, oh, I wouldn't – not for the world – are you sure?

BEAUTY. *(smiling at him)* Why, yes, I am quite sure.

GIRL'S VOICE. *(off left)* Fred!

YOUNG MAN. Oh, coming! *(explaining to BEAUTY)* My sister.

GIRL'S VOICE. Fred!

YOUNG MAN. Coming!

(The **YOUNG MAN** *goes off left, holding the ball, staring at* **BEAUTY** *with his head over his shoulder, and tripping over the ramp.* **BEAUTY** *bends and picks up a shell.)*

MRS. CRUM. George!

*(***GEORGE** *gives her a guilty look and pretends to read the newspaper, watching* **BEAUTY** *from behind it.* **BEAUTY** *exits right.)*

MOM. Those bikinis, as they call them. Didn't ought to be allowed. The Archbishop of Canterbury should preach against them.

MRS. CRUM. No *nice* girl would wear one.

*(***PERCY** *enters slowly left, depressed.)*

MOM. *(brightly)* Seen your friends off?

PERCY. *(sadly)* Yes, they've gone. *(He looks off left to the sea.)* I'll go and get your wool now. *(He starts up the ramp.)*

MOM. I think – after all – I shall have just enough.

GEORGE. You bloody well would have.

*(***MRS. CRUM** *glares at* **GEORGE** *and gives an embarrassed laugh to* **MOM.** **GEORGE** *rises, moves to the telescope right, focuses in the direction* **BEAUTY** *has gone, and takes some money from his pocket.)*

MRS. CRUM. Don't waste your money, George.

*(***GEORGE** *re-focuses the telescope.)*

GEORGE. There was a ship out there. No, dear. *(He sits.)*

MOM. You'd better have your afternoon dip, Percy.

PERCY. Don't think I want to. *(He crosses to right of the steps centre.)* It's turning cold. The sun's nearly off the beach.

MOM. Oh, but it's good for you, Percy. This is your holiday, you know. You want to enjoy yourself.

PERCY. Not much fun going in by yourself.

MOM. Now go along, dear. Needn't stop in long. The salt water's *good* for you.

(Morosely, **PERCY** *moves to near the deck-chair, taking off his shirt and trousers. He is wearing bathing costume underneath. The trousers lie close to those of* **BOB**.*)*

MOM. Put your things in the hut.

PERCY. *(still morose)* They're all right there. *(With his back to the ramp, he reaches for the towel on his chair.)*

*(***NOREEN** *rushes in from left, knocking* **PERCY** *over.* **BOB** *follows her on.)*

NOREEN. Oh, sorry, I'm sure. *(giving him a coquettish glance)* Never look where I'm going.

PERCY. That's all right.

NOREEN. It's lovely and warm.

BOB. Don't believe her, chum. It's freezing. *(He runs "on the spot," then dries himself.)*

*(***PERCY** *goes off left.)*

NOREEN. *(drying herself)* Oh, you! Soft – that's what you are.

BOB. *(crossing to her and showing his muscles)* Soft? Me? Feel those muscles.

*(***NOREEN** *drops her towel.* **BOB** *picks her up, twirls her round, and they sit,* **NOREEN** *left of the sand castle,* **BOB** *right of it.* **MOM** *and* **MRS. CRUM** *register aloof distaste.)*

NOREEN. *(kneeling, resting on* **MR. SOMERS**'s *knees)* Oh, I'm all dizzy.

BOB. Oh! I've done myself an injury! *(He lies on his towel, right of the sand castle, with his head up stage.)* How about a bit of sun on the body beautiful, eh? *(He beats a tattoo on his stomach.)*

*(*NOREEN *settles down on the sand.)*

MRS. CRUM. Mrs Gunner...

MOM. Pardon?

MRS. CRUM. Have you heard there was a burglary last night? That Lady Beckman who's always in the papers – the one with the minks – lost her emerald necklace.

MOM. I expect she took it herself – for the insurance. They're always doing that sort of thing.

GEORGE. Says in the paper here it was a cat burglar.

MRS. CRUM. These cat burglars go all round the seaside resorts in summer. Do you remember, George, there was a burglary here last year – and *that* was a cat burglar.

*(*BOB *sits up.)*

Some film star lost a diamond bracelet.

GEORGE. *(sleepily)* Don't remember.

MRS. CRUM. Oh, you must remember. It made ever such a stir. There were pictures of the window and the drainpipe and lots of pictures of her and bits about a new picture she was going to do.

GEORGE. *(closing his eyes)* Nice bit of publicity.

*(*BOB *teases* NOREEN *with a shell.)*

NOREEN. You leave me alone, you great bully! *(She circles the sand castle and trips over* MOM*'s feet.)* Oh, sorry, I'm sure.

MOM. I've dropped a stitch.

NOREEN. *(moving up the steps to* MOM*'s left)* Oh, I say – *(helpfully)* let me pick it up for you.

MOM. No, thank you.

NOREEN. Oh, go on. I'm ever so good at picking up stitches.

MOM. *(with venom)* No, certainly not.

BOB. *(kneeling on all fours facing* MOM*)* No harm in being civil, is there?

MOM. *(frostily)* I beg your pardon.

NOREEN. *(moving down the steps and across to* **MR. SOMERS***)* Leave it, Bob. Artie, got a cigarette? *(She takes two cigarettes from* **MRS SOMERS***'s packet and lights them both.)*

BOB. This place is like a bloomin' morgue. *(He rises, puts the bucket on his head, and does an Egyptian dance.)*

NOREEN. Here, Bob, sit down.

(A dog is heard barking.)

Have a cigarette.

*(***BOB** *takes a cigarette and sits as before.)*

MOTHER. *(off right)* Ernie! Ernie! You ain't half a naughty boy. Ernie!

(The dog stops barking.)

NOREEN. Wish I'd brought my transistor. We could have had a bit of Adam.

BOB. That stuff's on the way out. Give me the old minstrels. *(He sings.)*
OH, I DO LIKE TO BE BESIDE THE SEA SIDE –

NOREEN.
– I DO LIKE TO BE BESIDE THE SEA –

BOB.
I DO LIKE TO STROLL ALONG THE PROM – PROM – PROM –

NOREEN AND BOB. *(singing together)*
WHERE THE BRASS BAND PLAYS TIDDLEY-OM-POM-POM –

BOB.
– OH, I –

GEORGE. *(singing)*
– DO LIKE TO BE BESIDE THE SEASIDE! I DO LIKE...
(He breaks off.)

*(***MRS. CRUM** *glares at* **GEORGE**. *A jet plane passes over from left to right.)*

BOB. How'd you like to be up there, Noreen? Two-seater jet.

NOREEN. Don't talk so daft, Bob. You'd be scared to death. You know you would.

(**INSPECTOR FOLEY**, *a tall, uniformed figure, enters down right, followed by the* **BEACH ATTENDANT**.)

BOB. Scared? Scared be... (*He ad libs until* **NOREEN** *sees the* **INSPECTOR**.)

GEORGE. Why, it's Inspector Foley. Remember us from last year? Crum!

FOLEY. (*nodding to him*) Good afternoon, Mr. Crum – Mrs. Crum.

GEORGE. (*facetiously*) Well, how's crime?

FOLEY. Hoh! (*He crosses to centre, mounts the steps of Mon Desir, and moves to left of* **MRS. CRUM**.)

(*The* **BEACH ATTENDANT** *remains down right.*)

Or mustn't I ask, on your afternoon off?

MRS. CRUM. This is Inspector Foley, Mrs Gunner.

FOLEY. (*turning to* **MOM**) Good afternoon, madam. (*to* **GEORGE**) Unfortunately I'm *not* off duty, Mr. Crum.

GEORGE. (*taking off his spectacles*) Looking for cat burglars, is that it?

FOLEY. You're on the right track.

GEORGE. Doesn't seem much scope for them here. (*He looks at the huts.*)

FOLEY. Information received, it seems some kids were out after dark last night and were down on the beach playing cops and robbers, or spacemen and atom bombs or whatever kids do play nowadays, and they saw a man sneaking round the huts at this end of the Parade.

(**BOB** *nudges* **NOREEN**.)

I dare say they wouldn't have thought much of it but the man bolted when he saw them.

MRS. CRUM. I suppose he was trying to steal something out of the huts?

FOLEY. According to them, he was trying to shove something *into* a hut through the little back window. The kids only came clean about it this afternoon.

It might just possibly tie up with the theft of Lady Beckman's necklace. Passing it on to an accomplice.

BOB. Loverlee! *(putting his hands up)* Search me, Officer, I am innocent.

MR. SOMERS. Stop playing the fool, Bob.

BOB. Oh blimey, I thought you were dead. *(He turns to the others.)* I thought he was dead.

(NOREEN laughs.)

GEORGE. So you're searching all the huts?

FOLEY. Just the huts this end of the beach. We've done the first three. *(He points right.)* It definitely wasn't farther along than the sixth.

GEORGE. *(to MRS. CRUM)* Didn't notice an emerald necklace, did you, Mother, in our palatial establishment?

MRS. CRUM. Well, I never! Do you really think it might be in Bide-a-Wee? *(pleased and flustered)* We've got so much stuff in there that I mightn't have noticed it. You go in and have a good look round, Inspector.

FOLEY. *(coming down the steps of Mon Desir)* Thank you, Mrs. Crum.

GEORGE. Anything in it for us, if you find it?

FOLEY. *(mounting the steps of Bide-a-Wee, and going into the hut)* Reward of one thousand pounds offered by Sir Rupert Backman…

GEORGE. Not bad.

(PERCY enters down left and moves on to the ramp.)

BOB. Might be a prison sentence if it's found in your hut – receiving stolen goods.

MRS. CRUM. How dare you!

PERCY. What's going on?

BOB. Hello, old boy. We're all under suspicion – particularly those who own beach huts.

NOREEN. It's the emerald necklace that was stolen from Lady Beckman last night.

MRS. CRUM. Someone was seen pushing it through one of the hut windows.

GEORGE. They don't know it *was* the necklace.

BOB. Might have been a love letter, or obscene literature.

NOREEN. Really, Bob, your mind! *(She laughs.)*

(**BOB** *laughs.* **PERCY** *dries himself on his towel by his chair.)*

BOB. Anyway, old girl, we're in the clear. *(He looks at* **MRS. CRUM.***) We're* not one of the nobs with a beach hut. We don't belong to the marine aristocracy. We're just common or garden visitors – *(pointedly)* not good enough for some people.

BOB. *(using a shell as a monocle and mimicking a Mayfair accent)* If you don't have a hut at Little-Slippyng-on-Sea you're low common folk, not worth a civil word.

MOM. People who have gone to the expense of renting a beach hut here, expect to be able to sit in front of it in peace and quiet.

BOB. Ladi-bloomin'-da! *(facing* **MOM***)* What's wrong with people enjoying themselves?

MOM. This has always been a very select place.

PERCY. *(unhappily; leaning over to* **MOM***)* Look here, Mom, we don't want to say anything we don't mean. *(He smiles at* **BOB.***)* I'm sure we all want to just enjoy a nice holiday at the seaside. 　　　　　　　　　　 ·

(The **MOTHER** *enters right with a piece of seaweed and crosses to left.)*

BOB. *(sitting round front again; pacified)* Sure, chum. That's all right by me. What I said was just a bit of fun.

(As **MOTHER** *moves above* **NOREEN** *to exit left, the seaweed touches* **NOREEN** *'s back.)*

MOTHER. As soon as I touched my seaweed, I knew it was gonna be wet.

FOLEY. *(emerging from the hut to between* **GEORGE** *and* **MRS. CRUM***)* Well, Mrs. Crum, you're certainly very fully furnished, as the house agents say.

*(***PERCY** *goes into his hut.)*

MRS. CRUM. Bide-a-Wee's absolutely our home when we're here. I like nice things.

*(***GEORGE** *does a "winding-up" motion.)*

We can have tea here, or lunch. We've got a gramophone – and a portable wireless, and coats and mackintoshes, and sewing doings… *(She notices* **GEORGE***, and stops, glaring.)*

*(***GEORGE** *reads his paper.)*

FOLEY. Yes, indeed. Hardly got room to get inside yourselves. *(He descends the steps, signs to the* **BEACH ATTENDANT** *and crosses to below* **MOM***'s steps.)*

(The **BEACH ATTENDANT** *goes up* **BEAUTY***'s steps to right of* **MOM***.)*

BEACH ATTENDANT. *(reading from a paper)* Ben Nevis – Mrs Gunner – this lady.

*(***PERCY** *comes out of the hut.)*

FOLEY. Is this your hut, madam?

MOM. It certainly is.

FOLEY. Mind if I have a look inside?

MOM. *(belligerently)* Have you got a search warrant?

BOB. Oi! Oi!

FOLEY. *(his eyebrows rising)* No.

MOM. Then you'd better go and get one.

PERCY. I say, Mom…

MOM. Be quiet, Percy.

FOLEY. But really, madam, I cannot see why you should object to…

MOM. That Lady Beckman! With her mink coats and her Rolls Royce cars! Sending along policemen to poke and pry into people's private huts. It's disgraceful and I won't have it.

PERCY. But look here, Mom…

MOM. Will you be quiet, Percy.

BEACH ATTENDANT. *(suddenly coming forward to right of* **MOM** *and speaking persuasively)* Now, madam, be reasonable. It wouldn't be nice for a lady like you to be seen going to the police station with an officer in order to make a statement, and that's what will happen. Mr Foley here is a very nice gentleman and he just wants to satisfy himself as there's nothing there shouldn't be in your beach hut. Why, you know, Mum, it mightn't be an emerald necklace at all. For all you know, it might be a bomb.

*(***MOM*** is slightly shattered by the bomb theory. ***GEORGE*** lowers his paper. ***BOB*** laughs.)*

MOM. A bomb? But why?

BEACH ATTENDANT. You never know nowadays. *(looking at* **FOLEY***)* All this atomic stuff and Communists.

MOM. Very well. *(to* **FOLEY***; grandly)* You may enter, Inspector.

(The **BEACH ATTENDANT** *straightens up, descends the steps and crosses to below* **GEORGE***.* **FOLEY** *enters Ben Nevis.* **PERCY** *sits in his chair.)*

GEORGE. *(to the* **BEACH ATTENDANT***)* You're quite a one, aren't you?

BEACH ATTENDANT. *(picking up a carton and putting it in the bin down right)* Have to be, in my job. Trouble, trouble, all day long. The ladies are all right if you know how to treat'em. *(thoughtfully)* You see a lot of 'uman nature on the beach.

BOB. One thousand pounds reward! Phew! Worth having a shot at it. Good as winning a premium bond or the pools, eh, Artie?

(**FOLEY** *comes out from the hut and down the steps.*
BEAUTY *comes on down right by the telescope and stands*
watching.)

MR. SOMERS. You've got to have brains to do the pools.

(**FOLEY** *stops above* **NOREEN**.)

NOREEN. Coo – if I found an emerald necklace, I'd keep it.
(She sees **FOLEY**.*)* 'Ullo!

FOLEY. *(looking at the middle hut)* Mon Desir. *(He crosses to the*
rostrum.)

BEACH ATTENDANT. *(reading from his list)* Ben Nevis, Mrs
Gunner. Mong Desser.

(He mounts the steps of Mon Desir with **FOLEY**.)

Mrs Murgatroyd, not seen her about lately. Don't
suppose anyone's at home. *(He raps on the door.)*

(**BEAUTY** *comes down the steps right by the telescope.)*

BEAUTY. Ye-es? You want something please?

(**GEORGE** *looks at her.)*

I can do something?

MRS. CRUM. George!

BEACH ATTENDANT. This is Mrs Murgatroyd's hut?

BEAUTY. *(nodding vigorously, and coming below right of the steps*
of Mon Desir) Oh, yes. She is friend of my aunt's. She
say to me, I can use her hut. She give me ze key. *(She*
holds out the key, taking it from her bra.)

FOLEY. *(taking it)* Oh! I am Inspector Foley. Will you allow
me to inspect…

BEAUTY. You are inspector? Yes? You do not like my
costume? *(looking down at herself)* Is not enough? No?

GEORGE. Yes.

BOB. Mamselle, it's perfect.

BEACH ATTENDANT. It's not your costume, miss. We're
broad-minded here, not like some beaches. You see,
there has been a robbery, and the Inspector here

thinks – er – something may have been put in your hut.

BEAUTY. I do not understand. Who put in my hut? What?

GEORGE. An emerald necklace.

BEAUTY. An emerald necklace! In my hut? Why? C'n'est pas possible. Je ne pense pas comprendre. Qui l'aurait faite, une belle chose. Mais c'est completement fou.

GEORGE. Yes – well – er – yes.

FOLEY. Mademoiselle – vous – you permit me to enter?

BEAUTY. Oh, yes, I permit. (*She sits right of the steps of Mon Desir.*)

(**FOLEY** *enters Mon Desir.* **BEAUTY** *drops her sunglasses.* **PERCY** *retrieves them for her.*)

(*giving him a warm smile*) Oh, thank you. You are very kind.

PERCY. (*embarrassed and pleased*) Don't mention it. (*He sits left of the steps of Mon Desir.*)

BEAUTY. (*to* **PERCY**) You have been in the sea? It is very cold.

PERCY. No, not at all. I mean, yes, it is.

BEAUTY. But you are braver, perhaps, than I am. If the water is cold I am not brave.

(**FOLEY** *comes out to left of the hut. The* **BEACH ATTENDANT** *stands at right of him.*)

FOLEY. Not much in there.

BEAUTY. No, there is very little. Some very ugly cups and saucers and a tin of tea, and plain, plain English biscuits. I do not like your English biscuits.

MOM. (*to* **PERCY**; *sharply*) Percy, get your clothes on. You'll die of cold.

PERCY. (*Fascinated by* **BEAUTY**, *who is smiling at him?*) What? Oh, yes!

MR. SOMERS. Yes, it is getting chilly.

NOREEN. *(rising; sharply)* Well, if the excitement's over, what about a run along the beach? Coming, Bob? 'Bye, Arthur.

(NOREEN exits left.)

BOB. *(rising and turning to BEAUTY)* Well, au revoy, eh? *(Still watching BEAUTY, he starts crossing left.)*

(NOREEN returns down left. BOB bumps into her.)

NOREEN. Come on then, Bob!

BOB. *(reluctantly)* Coming. Just having a parlez-vous with this bird here…

NOREEN. Just 'cos she's French…!

(NOREEN pushes BOB, and they exit down left.)

FOLEY. Sorry you've been troubled.

(FOLEY exits up the ramp and to up left. MR. SOMERS rises with difficulty, using his sticks. The BEACH ATTENDANT crosses left to him.)

BEACH ATTENDANT. Give you a hand, sir?

MR. SOMERS. *(crossing right)* I can manage. *(He raises his hat when left of BEAUTY.)* Bon jour!

(MR. SOMERS exits down right. The BEACH ATTENDANT exits down left.)

BEAUTY. Poor man. *(She opens her cigarette-case and takes a cigarette out.)* Oh – please – will you be very kind?

PERCY. *(rising to left of BEAUTY)* Of course, yes, anything.

BEAUTY. My lighter, she has packed up.

(GEORGE rises, taking his lighter out. PERCY crosses to right of BEAUTY, takes GEORGE's lighter, and lights her cigarette.)

Thank you.

MOM. Get your clothes on, Percy. It's cold!

PERCY. My clothes? Oh – yes… *(He moves on to the rostrum to enter Ben Nevis.)*

GEORGE. Oi, Romeo! *(He holds out his hand.)*

(PERCY *dashes back, returns* GEORGE*'s lighter, crosses to the deck-chair, picks up* BOB*'s trousers and his own shirt, and goes into the hut, closing the door behind him.* GEORGE *sits again.* BEAUTY *hums a little tune.* GEORGE *watches her avidly.* MRS. CRUM *and* MOM *look at each other.* BEAUTY *looks at* GEORGE *and smiles.*)

MRS. CRUM. (*packing away her knitting and rising with determination*) Come on, George, we'll go along to the kiosk and have a cup of tea.

GEORGE. Don't think I want any tea.

MRS. CRUM. We'll go along to the kiosk and have a cup of tea, George.

GEORGE. Will we? All right, then.

(MRS. CRUM *leans on* GEORGE*'s knee to descend the steps.*)

Oh! Blimey!

MRS. CRUM. Give us a hand down, can't you?

(GEORGE *helps her down the steps. When she has passed* BEAUTY, MRS. CRUM *adjusts her girdle, and crosses on to the ramp.*)

(*from the ramp*) Are you coming, Mrs Gunner?

MOM. (*obviously longing for tea, but not wanting to leave* PERCY *and* BEAUTY *together*) Well, in a minute perhaps.

MRS. CRUM. The kiosk shuts at five.

BEAUTY. (*rising*) I think I shall go now and take a bath.

(BEAUTY *takes her bathing-cap and crosses to exit down left.* PERCY *comes out of the hut, wearing shirt and trousers, and stares after* BEAUTY.)

MOM. (*rising; sharply*) Mrs. Crum and I are going to have a cup of tea.

PERCY. Right you are. (*He moves down to the bottom of the ramp.*) I don't want any. I'll go for a stroll. (*He prepares to start after* BEAUTY.)

MOM. No, Percy, you'll stay here until we come back. Do you understand? Don't move from here. Anything might be taken.

(**PERCY** *moves centre, to right of the sand castle.*)

It's bad enough ordinary days, and with all these cat burglars and dangerous characters about, you can't be too careful. Look after Mr and Mrs. Crum's things too. Percy. Oh, all right.

(**GEORGE** *comes to behind* **PERCY**, *both looking after* **BEAUTY**.)

MOM. (*as she and* **MRS. CRUM** *move up the ramp*) I'm not going to that place we went to yesterday. My cup was covered in lipstick. I didn't like the girl, either.

(**MOM** *and* **MRS. CRUM** *go off up left.* **GEORGE** *moves after them, but turns first and winks at* **PERCY**.)

GEORGE. Good luck, my boy.

(**PERCY** *looks at him miserably.* **GEORGE** *moves to the ramp, looks off up left, then returns to left of* **PERCY**. *The light starts to fade a little.*)

Look here, Percy, my boy, you stand up for yourself before it's too late.

PERCY. What do you mean?

GEORGE. There's such a thing as being *too* nice to your mother. All very well in its way, but you can go too far. Assert yourself. Be a man.

MRS. CRUM. (*off*) George!

GEORGE. Coming!

(**GEORGE** *exits up left.* **PERCY** *sits by himself on the beach, staring miserably in front of him. He feels in his right-hand trouser pocket for a cigarette, then, still abstractedly, in his left-hand pocket. He frowns, feeling with his fingers, and slowly draws out a gleaming emerald necklace. He stares at it for a moment uncomprehendingly, then a look of horror passes over his face. He looks sharply up and down the beach, shoves the*

necklace back in his pocket, takes it out again, and stares
at it. Then he rises, goes up the ramp left, returns to the
beach, looks off left, and looks at Mon Desir.)

NOREEN. *(off left)* Come on, Bob, don't take all day.

BOB. *(off left)* I've dropped me towel.

(**PERCY** *shoves the necklace back in his pocket and sits*
centre abruptly. **NOREEN** *enters down left.)*

NOREEN. C'mon, I'll beat you, Bob. You're out of condition.
Too many cigarettes.

BOB. *(off left)* Only forty a day.

(**PERCY** *kneels on the sand.)*

NOREEN. Blimey, I'm out of breath!

(**PERCY** *does not answer. She looks at him.)*

Hullo – anything the matter?

PERCY. No – yes.

NOREEN. *(left of* **PERCY***)* Well, make up your mind. I'd
better get dressed, I suppose. *(She goes to the sand castle*
for her towel, then faces the rostrum centre.) Dressing and
undressing on a beach is a regular art, I must say. At
the critical moment the towel always slips. *(She slips her*
shoulder-straps off and tucks the towel under her arms.)

(**BOB** *enters left, panting.)*

BOB. Oh!

NOREEN. Go away, Bob. You'll have to wait until I'm Mrs
Respectable. At the moment I'm liable to be Mrs Rude
any minute.

BOB. Pardon me, I'm sure. Sing out when you're decent.
Where's old Arthur? Oh, I see him, doing his
constitutional over there.

(**BOB** *crosses and exits down right.)*

PERCY. *(to himself)* Wish I knew what to do.

NOREEN. Pardon? *(letting the towel slip off her left shoulder)*
Oh, drat this towel. You – Mister...

PERCY. Percy Gunner.

NOREEN. Yes, hang on! *(She holds out the end of the towel.)*

*(**PERCY** takes it, right of her.)*

That's it, just keep it from slipping. *(She wriggles a good deal. The towel slips.)* Where's me clothes? *(She moves above the deck-chair, picks up her dress and places it on the rostrum.)* Where's me... *(She goes to her beach bag above the deck-chair.)* Bra! Bra! Bra! *(She takes out her bra, crosses and puts it on top of her dress.)* Oh, here, give it to me. *(She takes the towel from **PERCY**.)* You must keep watch. *(She starts to dry herself, then notices **PERCY** watching her.)* Well, don't watch *me!* Watch out for men.

*(**PERCY** moves right centre, looking off right.)*

(She dries herself, then takes her bra and shakes it.) Blimey, it's full of sand! *(She puts on her bra.)* Can't find the bloomin' hook. Here, Percy, hang on. Both ends. *(giving him the towel)*

*(**PERCY** holds the towel, facing front.)*

(She fastens the hook, and slips into her dress. Then she steps out from behind the towel.) Olé!

*(**PERCY** drops the towel.)*

NOREEN. *(turning to face left)* Zip me up, ducks, will you?

*(**PERCY** goes to her and tries to zip the dress.)*

Wicked things, zips. Here, take it by surprise.

*(**PERCY** zips the dress.)*

Don't forget the hook at the top.

*(**PERCY** fastens the hook at the top of the dress.)*

Not very used to this sort of thing, are you? You're looking very serious! Anything the matter? *(She struggles out of her costume.)*

PERCY. Wish I knew what to do.

NOREEN. Where's me Kleenex? *(She drops the costume on the sand, goes to her handbag, kneels, takes out a Kleenex, and blows her nose.)* Now, what's the matter with you, ducks?

(She takes a mirror and comb from her bag and combs her hair.)

PERCY. *(moving to right of* NOREEN *and showing her the necklace)* Look! I've just found this in my trouser pocket.

NOREEN. *(stopping combing and staring at it)* What on earth – you mean – is this the necklace that all the fuss is about?

PERCY. I should think it must be. Don't you?

NOREEN. And you found it in your – what do you mean, *found* it? Didn't you know it was there?

PERCY. I hadn't the least idea.

NOREEN. You mean, you didn't put it there yourself?

PERCY. Of course I didn't! It wasn't there just now – before I went to bathe.

NOREEN. You mean – someone put it there.

PERCY. They must have.

NOREEN. But who? But who? *(She gives a sharp glance round at the huts and the beach.)* Oh, I see…

PERCY. What d'you mean?

NOREEN. *(going to her beach bag and taking out her drawers)* Where's me drawers? *(shaking them)* Sand everywhere! *(She puts them on.)*

(The YOUNG MAN *enters down left with the ball as* NOREEN *has her drawers round her ankles. He whistles and exits left.* NOREEN *turns right as* PERCY *is watching.* PERCY *turns right, while* NOREEN *faces up stage and pulls up her drawers.)*

PERCY. You said "you see." What do you see?

NOREEN. *(slowly, as though trying to puzzle something out, as she kneels by the sand castle and combs her hair)* Of course. *She* must have put it there.

PERCY. She? You mean…

NOREEN. The Pin-up Girl from Mon Desir.

PERCY. No! I don't believe it.

NOREEN. Only way it could have happened. Your clothes were on the beach, weren't they? The police came along. I suppose she had it with her in that bathing bag. When they started to search your hut, she shoved it in your trouser pocket.

PERCY. Yes – yes – I suppose that's how it must have happened.

NOREEN. Well, cheer up. *(She drops the comb and rises to left of* **PERCY**.*)* 'Ere, you take it along to the inspector chap and you'll get the reward – a thousand pounds, just think of that.

PERCY. And she'll go to prison.

NOREEN. Oh, I see. *(She thumps him on the chest.)* Don't you be a sucker, Percy. That girl must be in with the gang. The cat burglar steals the things and shoves it in the hut, and she comes along and picks it up next day.

PERCY. *(unwillingly)* Yes, I suppose it must have been like that. *(Looking off down left.)* But she's so young.

NOREEN. Probably been at it ever since she was a kiddy. Their mums teach 'em to shoplift when they're children.

*(***BOB*** enters down left and goes to above the deck-chair for his sweater.)*

BOB. *(crossly)* Don't care if I die of cold, do you? Why didn't you shout when you were ready?

NOREEN. Bob, you'll never guess! What d'you think Mister – Percy…?

PERCY. Percy Gunner.

NOREEN. What d'you think he's got? *(She takes the necklace from* **PERCY** *and crosses to right of* **BOB**.*)* Hold your breath, count three, and don't say anything you'd be sorry for afterwards. *(She holds up the necklace.)*

(As ***BOB****'s head comes through his sweater he sees the necklace.)*

BOB. *(bereft of speech for a moment)* Well – blimey! Cor stone the crows! Where did that come from?

NOREEN. Found it in his trouser pocket, see? I tell him someone must have put it there.

BOB. *(a little dazed)* Someone must have put it there – who?

NOREEN. The girl, of course. The foreign girl. It couldn't have been anyone else. You agree, don't you? It must have been that girl.

BOB. *(sitting in the deck-chair and combing his hair)* Oh, yes, undoubtedly – the girl.

PERCY. *(explosively)* No!

BOB. *(looking at PERCY as he parts his hair)* But it stands to reason, old man.

PERCY. No – I don't believe it. I won't believe it!

NOREEN. *(moving to left of PERCY)* You men – you're all the same. Here she is – coming now. *(She moves above the deck-chair.)*

(BEAUTY enters left. She is not wet. She crosses to PERCY. PERCY puts her cape on.)

BEAUTY. *(smiling)* Oh, thank you. It is cold, the water, I put one toe in, so – *(she demonstrates)* and I say *no!* I... *(She stops as she sees the necklace. There is a pause, then she goes on with a slight change of voice.)* Ah, you have my necklace there.

BOB. Are you telling us that's yours?

BEAUTY. But yes – of course!

PERCY. But – it was stolen.

BEAUTY. *(laughing)* Ah – I see. You think it is *that* necklace. No, it is mine. It is – how do you say – costume jewellery. *(She crosses to NOREEN and takes the necklace from her quickly. She clasps it round her neck, and turns to PERCY.)* It looks nice, yes? *(She turns to NOREEN.)* Where did you find it?

PERCY. It was in my pocket.

BEAUTY. *(surprised) In your* pocket? You took it? But why?

PERCY. I didn't take it.

BEAUTY. *(gently)* I see. You did not know you took it. Yes, I have heard of that – klop – m – kleptomania. You cannot help it. See, I have my necklace back and nothing more shall be said about it. *(She goes up the centre steps on to the rostrum.)*

BOB. *(sharply and with an ugly manner)* No!

(BEAUTY stops and turns enquiringly.)

No, you don't. *(He rises and goes on to the rostrum, left of BEAUTY.)*

BEAUTY. What do you want?

BOB. You're not going to get away with that necklace.

PERCY. *(suddenly looking down at his legs)* Wait a minute! These aren't my trousers. *(He crosses to the deck-chair.)* I had cigarettes in my trousers. *(to BOB)* Those are my trousers. These are yours. It was in your pocket.

BOB. *(menacingly; to BEAUTY)* Hand that over – quick.

BEAUTY. No, I will not.

(PERCY advances on him. BOB snatches the necklace from BEAUTY and runs down on to the beach. BEAUTY trips him up and he falls on the sand down right, dropping the necklace. FOLEY enters down right to above right of BOB. MR. SOMERS enters down right to right of BOB. NOREEN crosses to left of FOLEY, who picks up the necklace. PERCY crosses to below left of NOREEN. BEAUTY comes down the centre steps.)

FOLEY. Keep him there!

(Characters speak simultaneously.)

BOB. Oh, my knee! I've broken something!

BEAUTY. *(speaking now without a foreign accent)* It was in his trouser pocket. The other gentleman put the wrong trousers on.

PERCY. I picked up the wrong trousers.

MR. SOMERS. What's going on here?

NOREEN. I don't understand – what's happening?

(End of simultaneous speech.)

NOREEN. Arthur, it's the necklace. Lady Beckman's, the stolen one. It seems to have been in Bob's pocket.

BOB. It's a frame-up, I tell you.

NOREEN. I can't believe it. I just can't believe it.

MR. SOMERS. Bob?

FOLEY. *(to NOREEN)* How well do you know this man?

MR. SOMERS. Only met him since we came down here – a week ago.

NOREEN. Staying at the same guest-house.

MR. SOMERS. Seemed a very pleasant, agreeable chap. We've got in the habit of going about together.

FOLEY. Just so.

NOREEN. I can't believe it. Bob – a cat burglar.

BOB. *(rising)* It's all a mistake, I tell you! Someone put that necklace in my pocket. It's a frame-up.

FOLEY. You can explain all that at the station. Get your clothes!

(**BOB** *rises and crosses to above the deck-chair.* **FOLEY** *moves to above the sand castle, patting* **PERCY** *on the back in passing.*)

Good piece of work, my boy. Looks as though you may be the richer by a thousand pounds.

BOB. These aren't my trousers.

PERCY. Wait a minute. *(He takes off the trousers he is wearing.)*

FOLEY. *(handing* **BOB**'*s shoes to him, and taking the trousen from him)* Are these your shoes?

PERCY. *(holding up the trousers in front of him)* You do understand, don't you, that this young lady had nothing whatever to do with it? Excuse me!

FOLEY. *(grinning)* I'd better introduce you.

(**GEORGE** *and* **MRS. CRUM** *enter up left and move to the foot of the ramp.*)

This is Policewoman Alice Jones.

(PERCY drops the trousers. FOLEY and PERCY exchange the trouser pairs via BEAUTY.)

·   Good work, Jones. You tripped him very neatly.

BEAUTY. Thank you, sir.

FOLEY. On your way!

BOB. French policewoman on an English beach. I'll see my shop steward about this!

(FOLEY and BOB exit by the ramp up left.)

PERCY. Policewoman Alice Jones!

BEAUTY. Yes.

MR. SOMERS. *(crossing below PERCY and BEAUTY to sit in the deck-chair)* You could have fooled me.

PERCY. You were on duty?

BEAUTY. Yes.

PERCY. You – you don't look like a policewoman.

(NOREEN crosses between PERCY and BEAUTY to left of the sand castle, kneels, and collects her things.)

BEAUTY. I'm not supposed to.

PERCY. And what do you do next?

BEAUTY. Well – I've got the rest of the day off.

PERCY. Look here – would – could you – come and have something to eat at the Pavilion and then go to a show afterwards?

BEAUTY. I'd love to.

(MOM enters, to the up left edge of the rostrum.)

I'll just get some clothes on. *(She enters her hut to dress and closes the door.)*

PERCY. Oh, yes! *(He puts on his trousers.)*

MRS. CRUM. *(crossing to right of MOM's chair)* That girl – she's a policewoman!

MOM. *(going to her chair)* Percy, what is all this? What has been going on?

PERCY. I've recovered Lady Beckman's emerald necklace.

MRS. CRUM. Well, would you believe it?

GEORGE. *(crossing below the rostrum to his steps)* So you recovered it, did you? That's a thousand pounds in your pocket, me boy. Hope you're allowed to spend it.

MOM. A thousand pounds.

GEORGE. *(sitting in* **MRS. CRUM***'s chair)* Nothing like a bit of money to give you independence.

PERCY. It's not the money I'm thinking about. It's Miss...

MOM. Percy, what did you say to that girl?

PERCY. I asked her to go to the Pavilion with me.

MOM. Nonsense. You can't do that. You don't know her.

PERCY. I'll know her better soon.

GEORGE. I bet you will.

MRS. CRUM. George!

> *(***PERCY*** *moves up the ramp left.)*

MOM. Oh, dear! This has all been too much for me, I think I've got one of my headaches coming on. *(She sinks onto her chair.)*

> *(***MRS. CRUM*** *snatches* **MOM***'s knitting from her chair just before she sits on it.)*

MRS. CRUM. Whoops!

NOREEN. We'd better go home. *(She moves below* **MR. SOMERS** *on to the ramp.)* Bob a cat burglar! I can't believe it. Coming, Arthur?

MR. SOMERS. In a minute, dear. You go on.

NOREEN. *(nudging* **PERCY***)* Here, Percy, you know what you've got to do. Stick to your guns, Gunner!

> *(***NOREEN*** *exits up the ramp to up left.)*

MRS. CRUM. Come and see to your mother, Percy. She looks real bad to me.

PERCY. *(moving to left of* **MOM***)* Are you all right, Mom?

MOM. It's my heart.

GEORGE. Here we go again.

PERCY. Where are your smelling salts? *(He takes the salts from her bag and thrusts them under her nose.)*

*(**MOM** waves the salts away.)*

GEORGE. Here, fan her with this.

*(**PERCY** crosses to take **GEORGE**'s paper and fans **MOM**'s right ear, which she covers. Then he crosses to left of her. The **MOTHER** enters right, crossing to left.)*

MOTHER. Ernie! Bert! Come along the two of you, we've got to catch our bus.

MOM. Oh, that woman!

MOTHER. Ernie!

MOM. That voice!

MOTHER. I won't 'alf give it to you when I get hold of you. Ernie!!!

*(The **MOTHER** exits left. **BEAUTY** comes out of the hut.)*

BEAUTY. All ready now.

PERCY. I'm sorry – it's…

*(**BEAUTY** closes the door of the hut.)*

I mean – my mother isn't feeling very well.

MOM. I'm sorry to be such a drag on you, my dear boy, but I really feel *quite* queer.

PERCY. *(stopping fanning)* Perhaps – *(looking appealingly at* **MRS. CRUM***)* you'd be kind enough to… *(He stops.)*

MOM. *(to **BEAUTY**)* You'll understand I'm sure, Miss – er…

BEAUTY. Jones. Alice Jones.

MOM. Miss Jones. I'm so sorry – but I really have a very bad headache and I feel rather faint.

*(**PERCY** fans again.)*

BEAUTY. *(briskly)* That's too bad, isn't it. I know just what you need – rest. Men are useless when you're feeling ill, aren't they? *(She crosses down the steps to the ramp.)* Come on, Percy, we'll leave your mother to be peaceful.

PERCY. Mom…

MOM. Oh, dear. *(She closes her eyes.)*

BEAUTY. *(to **PERCY**)* Well? *(She waits.)*

PERCY. I…

BEAUTY. Well, good-bye, all. *(She goes up the ramp.)*

> *(**BEAUTY** exits up left.)*

PERCY. Wait! Miss Jones… *(He gives the paper to **MRS. CRUM**.)*

> *(**PERCY** exits up the ramp up left.)*

GEORGE. Good boy! Oh, good boy!

> *(**MRS. CRUM** sits in **PERCY**'s chair and fans **MOM**.)*

MOM. That I should ever live to see this day. My own boy going off and leaving me in that callous way. That horrid girl. Policewoman indeed.

MRS. CRUM. *(fanning herself)* Poor dear, I feel for you. I really do.

MOM. *(rising)* Well, I'm not going to sit around. I shall go home – if I can make it on my own.

MRS. CRUM. *(rising to left of her chair)* I'll come with you.

MOM. Leaving me to close up Ben Nevis on my own, too. I'm not used to it.

MRS. CRUM. George!

> *(**GEORGE** puts down his paper and crosses to stow away the chairs into Ben Nevis.)*

MOM. It's not a bit like my Percy. I don't know what's come over him.

GEORGE. *(folding the chairs)* I do.

MOM. See that everything's in.

> *(**GEORGE** puts away the second chair, crosses to his own chair, and picks up his paper.)*

If you'd be so kind, Mr. Crum.

> *(**GEORGE** crosses back, takes the key from **MOM** and locks the hut.)*

Have you locked up properly?

GEORGE. Here's your key. *(He gives her the key.)* I suppose we'd better take you home.

MOM. Oh, yes, take me home. *(She goes up the ramp.)*

(MRS. CRUM follows.)

Everybody knows I might die any minute. Nobody cares whether I live or die.

MRS. CRUM. No, George, we don't need you.

(MRS. CRUM and MOM exit up left.)

GEORGE. *(crossing along the rostrum to his hut)* Women!

MR. SOMERS. As you say – women.

*(GEORGE packs up his chairs and places them in the hut. The **BEACH ATTENDANT** enters down left, crosses to down right, picks up a carton and puts it in the basket, discovers a bra, picks it up, notices **GEORGE** has put his chairs in the hut and is about to descend his steps.)*

BEACH ATTENDANT. Wireless says it's gonna rain tomorrow. They'll be wrong. Never known them right yet. Be another blasted fine day.

GEORGE. *(looking at the bra)* Not mine.

*(The **BEACH ATTENDANT** exits down left. **GEORGE** crosses to right of the sand castle.)*

MR. SOMERS. Ah, well! *(He rises, stretches his legs, goes to the sand castle, extracts the necklace from it and hands it to **GEORGE**.)*

Here you are, old man.

GEORGE. So you had it all the time! But what was the other one?

MR. SOMERS. Oh, that was the replica. No time to leave it last night. Blasted chambermaid came along two hours after she was supposed to go off duty. Putting it in Bob's pocket was Noreen's little bit of fun.

GEORGE. Noreen's sense of fun will go too far one day. Poor old Bob.

MR. SOMERS. Well, somebody's got to be the fall guy. A good deal too fresh for my liking. Needs to be taught a lesson. He's cut out for the part. *(He moves to above the deck-chair.)* He's got a record, you know.

GEORGE. Whereas we – I'm a respectable working jeweller. Don't look like a fence, do I?

MR. SOMERS. And I don't look like a cat burglar, do I? *(He sits in the deck-chair.)*

(GEORGE goes to his hut to close the doors and lock up.)

MRS. CRUM. *(off)* George!

(MRS. CRUM enters up left.)

Come on, George. Are you going to stay on the beach all night? That Mrs Gunner's in a terrible state.

GEORGE. *(locking the hut)* Serve the old trout right.

MRS. CRUM. Eh? I tell you one thing. *(She moves to left of the rostrum.)* I'm not coming back to this place next year.

GEORGE. *(ambling after her)* Perhaps you're right, dear. Mustn't go to the same place too often.

MR. SOMERS. Excuse me, have you got a light?

(GEORGE comes down to the beach and lights a cigarette for MR. SOMERS.)

MRS. CRUM. Next year I shall go to Clacton-on-Sea.

(MRS. CRUM exits up left.)

GEORGE. Clacton-on-Sea. Yes, I think you've got something there. Clacton. Yes, that will do very nicely.

(GEORGE exits up left. MR. SOMERS crosses his game leg, and tilts his hat. The lights dim to a black-out.)

(curtain)

SET DESIGN

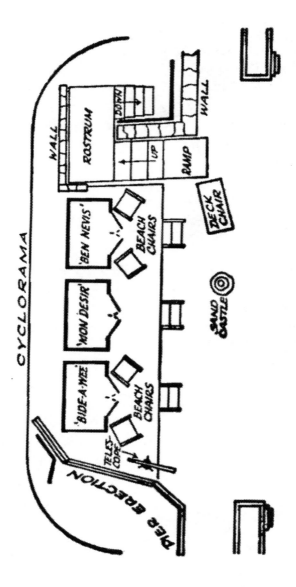

FURNITURE AND PROPERTY PLOT

Onstage:

Bide-a-Wee:

> *Top shelf:*
>
>> 3 boxes, flask, Frugrains, Ovaltine, blue tin, paintbrush, saucers, box
>
> *Lower shelf:*
>
>> Jug, plates, cups, bowl, saucers, jam, coffee, tins, cigarette packet, glass, jug, mayonnaise, cutlery, roses, paper bag, teapot, Silvikrin, glass, boxes, rusks, battery and flex
>
> *Line right:*
>
>> Tablecloth, left: bra, 2 scarves
>
> *On hooks:*
>
>> Tea-towel, carrier bag, mackintosh
>
> *On floor:*
>
>> Washing-bowl, box, towel-rail, hat, 2 tins of paint, 2 pairs of shoes, paper bags
>
> *In front:*
>
>> 2 camp-chairs, knitting bag left, newspaper right
>>
>> Doors, open
>>
>> Padlock on right door

Mon Desir:

> *Left side:*
>
>> Hooks, mirror (for quick change)
>
> *Top shelf:*
>
>> Magazine, tin, 5 books
>
> *Lower shelf:*
>
>> Pad, 3 saucers, teapot, 3 cups (hanging)
>
> *On floor:*
>
>> Broken camp-chair
>>
>> Doors, closed
>>
>> Padlock, open

Ben Nevis:

> *Left side:*
>
>> 2 camp-chairs, necklace on hook downstage corner
>
> *Top shelf:*
>
>> Jug, ball, saucepan, bowl, 2 saucers, 2 sweet boxes
>
> *On wall:*
>
>> Postcard

On hooks:

Tea-towel, 2 cups

On floor:

2 boxes, magazine, red socks

Doors, closed with padlock, but not snapped shut

Deck-chair down left.

> *On it:* newspaper, stick
>
> *Behind it:* Noreen's dress, Bob's trousers, sweater and comb

Sand castle down centre

> *In it:* necklace
>
> *On it:* rubber bucket, box with one chocolate
>
> *Left of it:* red towel, Noreen's shoes, pink bag with pants and bra, bathing cap, handbag with Kleenex, mirror, comb
>
> *Right of it:* Bob's towel, shoes, rubber shell, 2 shells

Telescope right. *On it:* litter basket (¾ full)

In right wing:

Bra, two pieces of rubbish

Offstage left:

Beach ball, Percy's towel

Offstage right:

Seaweed

On kiosk left:

> *Upstage flap:* postcards
>
> *Downstage flap:* 2 balls, 4 buckets; 5 spades

Personal:

Lighter (GEORGE)

Beach bag with sun-glasses, packet with 2 cigarettes (plain), lighter (no flint), bathing cap, key to Mon Desir (BEAUTY)

Bag with knitting, handbag with smelling-salts, key to Ben Nevis (MOM)

Packet with 3 cigarettes, matches, florin (MR. SOMERS)

Handbag (MRS. CRUM)

Tickets, ticket-clipper, money bag with 2 pennies, sixpence, shilling, hut list, whistle, watch and chain (BEACH ATTENDANT)

LIGHTING PLOT

Property fittings required: none
Exterior. A beach, a summer afternoon. The apparent source of light is the sun. The main acting areas are up right centre, up centre, up left centre, right centre, centre and left centre

To open: Black-out
Cue 1:
  At rise of curtain
  Fade up daylight
Cue 2:
  GEORGE: "Good luck, my boy."
  Daylight fades a little

Cue 3:
  At end of Play
  Dim to black-out

EFFECTS PLOT

Cue 1:
  BOB: "Keep Britain tidy."
  Jet plane flying overhead running into:
  Barking dog
Cue 2
  YOUNG MAN: "Sorry, sorry."
  Fade barking dog
Cue 3
  NOREEN: "Here, Bob, sit down."
  Dogfight
Cue 4
  MOTHER: "...a naughty boy. Ernie!"
  Dogfight stops
Cue 5
  GEORGE: "...beside the seaside."
  Jet plane flying overhead, roars twice then fast fade to out

The Rats

THE RATS was first presented by Peter Saunders at the Duchess Theatre, London, on 20th December 1962. The performance was directed by Hubert Gregg, with sets by Peter Rice. The cast was as follows:

SANDRA GREY	Betty McDowall
JENNIFER BRICE	Mercy Haystead
DAVID FORRESTER	David Langton
ALEC HANBURY	Raymond Bowers

CHARACTERS

SANDRA GREY
JENNIFER BRICE
DAVID FORRESTER
ALEC HANBURY

SETTING

The Michael Torrances' flat in Hampstead

(Scene: The Michael Torrances' flat in Hampstead. A fine summer evening about 6.30 P.M.)

(The flat is of the one-roomed modern type. A long window runs right across the back showing a view over the roof-tops. At the right of the window a door leads out to a small balcony. There is a door up left leading to the bathroom and kitchenette. The entrance door to the flat is down right. In the middle of the window centre is a very big chest of the type known as a Kuwait Bride Chest, dark wood studded with brass nails and ornamental hammered brass and copper. Prominent is a line of Baghdad coffee-pots with large spouts (beaked). There are one or two pieces of Persian or Islamic pottery, a Kurdish knife and Baghdad sugar hammer about. Otherwise the furnishing of the flat is severely modern. A big double divan, covered with cushions, is left, and a low plywood table right centre with light modern armchairs either side of it. On the table is a tray with drinks and a few glasses. There is a pouffe down centre and a budgerigar in a cage up centre. Modernistic patterned rugs are on the floor.)

(When the curtain rises, the room is empty. The lights fade up from black-out. Then a buzzer and knocker sound on the door right. This is repeated impatiently. Then **SANDRA**'s *voice cries out.)*

SANDRA. Anyone there? Anyone at home? *(She knocks on the door and gives a surprised exclamation as it opens.)*

*(**SANDRA** enters right. She is a smart and very attractive woman of thirty, conscious of her own sensual attractions.)*

Pat – Michael? *(She crosses above the table to the door left, exits, re-enters, crosses back to the door right, looks out, moves to the terrace and looks over the balcony. Then she moves back to behind the chair left centre, puts her wrap over the back of it, sits down on the chair left centre, takes off her gloves and puts them in her handbag. She reaches for the cigarette-box on the coffee-table, finds it empty and replaces it. She takes a cigarette-case and lighter from her handbag, lights a cigarette, replaces the case and lighter in the bag and places the bag on her chair.)* How extraordinary! *(She gets up and walks about, puffing nervously with increasing irritability and glancing at her watch.)* Nice manners, I must say. *(She goes on to the terrace.)*

(There is the sound of a key in the lock of the door right, trying to turn it. Then **JENNIFER** *speaks outside in a surprised voice.)*

JENNIFER. Oh, it's open! *(She pushes the door and enters.)*

*(***JENNIFER** *is a vacant-faced young woman of thirty-odd, a bit of a cat and not so silly as she seems. She has rather an affected manner. She takes her key out of the Yale lock, puts it in her handbag, crosses above the chairs, sees the wrap, stops and turns towards the terrace.)*

Hello, Sandra.

SANDRA. *(re-entering the room)* Jennifer – haven't seen you for ages.

JENNIFER. What are you doing here?

SANDRA. I'm like you – too early for the party. *(She crosses to the chair right.)* It's always so shaming to be early, isn't it? *(She sits.)*

JENNIFER. What's this about a party? Whose party?

SANDRA. Well, not a party exactly. The Torrances just said come in for drinks.

JENNIFER. *(surprised, moving between the chairs)* They asked you in for drinks *today?*

SANDRA. Why not? *(sharply)* Isn't that why you're here?

JENNIFER. Not exactly. *(She turns away, amused.)*

SANDRA. Why shouldn't the Torrances ask me in for drinks?

JENNIFER. *(crossing to the right edge of the divan)* No reason at all – *(She pauses.)* if they'd been in England.

SANDRA. Do you mean they're not in England?

JENNIFER. Unhmm. *(She nods.)* They're at Juan. *(She places her bag on the divan and sits at the right end of it.)*

SANDRA. But Pat Torrance rang me up on Tuesday, the day before yesterday.

JENNIFER. *(mockingly)* Did she?

SANDRA. *(sharply)* Yes.

JENNIFER. *(coolly)* Oh, really, darling! You must do better than that. It's never any good sticking to a story that won't gel.

SANDRA. Really, Jennifer!

JENNIFER. *(laughing)* I suppose you got Pat Torrance to lend you the key of the flat. *(She eyes her keenly.)* And you're meeting someone here! Who is it? You might tell me. Or shall I try and guess?

SANDRA. You're talking absolute nonsense. I told you, Pat Torrance rang me and asked me to come...

JENNIFER. *(picking up her bag)* Oh, darling! *Not* all over again! Think of something better. *(She looks at the cage.)* Perhaps she asked you to come in and feed the budgerigar?

SANDRA. *(doubtfully, sitting forward in her chair)* As a matter of fact – she – she did mention...

JENNIFER. *(laughing)* But I'd already agreed to feed the little brute for her. *(She takes a packet out of her bag, rises, and crosses to left of* SANDRA. *Reading the label:)* "Lovabud Budgie Food. Your Budgie will simply love it." *(She looks at the cage, then mockingly at* SANDRA.*)* How forgetful of Pat to ask two of us to do the same thing.

*(*SANDRA *rises, picks up her wrap and bag, crosses to left of the divan, and puts the bag down on it.)*

SANDRA. *(angrily)* Oh, really, Jennifer...

JENNIFER. Oh, don't be cross. I'm only teasing. It's so lovely, catching one's friends out. *(She crosses to the coffee-table and sits on the left end of it.)* But you might just tell me who he is. I swear I'll be as silent as the grave.

SANDRA. *(flicking her cigarette ash into the ashtray on the cabinet)* That'll be the day!

JENNIFER. Now, don't lose your temper, sweetie. What really surprises me is that the Torrances should aid and abet. I've always found them rather straight-laced. I put it down to living abroad so much in remote outposts of what used to be Empire. *(She rises, kneels on the pouffe left centre and goes on coaxingly.)* Sweetie, do tell me who it is you're having an affair with.

SANDRA. *(turning to JENNIFER)* I'm not having an affair with anyone.

JENNIFER. Then why are you here in the Torrances' flat when they're in the South of France – telling silly fibs about a cocktail party?

SANDRA. There must have been some mix-up or other – you know how things are on the telephone. Perhaps Pat meant *next* week. *(She crosses above JENNIFER to the chair right.)* But I can tell you that I came here expecting to find a party and that's all there is to it.

JENNIFER. *(disappointedly, sitting on the pouffe and facing SANDRA)* And you're really and truly not expecting to meet anyone here?

SANDRA. *(turning to face JENNIFER)* The only person I'm actually expecting to meet here is John.

JENNIFER. Your husband?

SANDRA. *(flicking her ash into the tray on the coffee-table)* Yes, He said he'd join me here as soon as he could get away from the office.

JENNIFER. Dear John. Such a pet, isn't he?

SANDRA. *(smiting as she sits in the chair right)* Naturally I think so.

JENNIFER. Such a nice, simple, *trusting* man! He simply worships you, doesn't he?

SANDRA. He doesn't actually dislike me.

JENNIFER. What splendid understatement! Men don't usually dislike you, do they? Quite the contrary.

SANDRA. *(coldly)* Hadn't you better feed the budgerigar if that's really what you've come for?

JENNIFER. *(rising to left of* **SANDRA***)* Sandra! Are you suggesting that I came here to meet someone?

SANDRA. Certainly not! I should never dream of such a thing.

JENNIFER. Well, that really is a bitchy thing to say! *(She moves up to the cage, sits on the chest, opens the cage door, takes out the tray, closes the door, and fills the tray from her packet.)* Tweet, tweet, tweet, here you are, then! Luvabud for the budgie. You know, there's something rather non-U about a budgie, don't you agree? But then there's something terribly non-U about the Torrances. All this travelling about to strange places and bringing back souvenirs. I stole an ashtray from the Carlton in Cannes once, but I never forgave myself. *(She replaces the seed tray and closes the cage.)* And why only one bird, why not two? Look at the poor little mite, all shut up in one room and simply pining for a mate. *(She looks at* **SANDRA***.)* But then, if there were two of you, you'd have to be faithful, wouldn't you? Such a bore. My God, he's drunk his own weight in water since this morning. *(She opens the cage, removes the water dish, closes the cage and moves to the door left.)* Never mind, Mother will get you some more – or do you suppose he'd rather have gin? If it is a he! *(She looks back at the cage.)* How do you tell?

*(***JENNIFER*** exits left. ***SANDRA*** rises and moves to the terrace. ***JENNIFER*** re-enters, having piled the water dish. She replaces it in the cage and closes the door, then picks up the seed packet from the chest.)*

What are you doing out there, darling? No good looking for the Torrances. I tell you they're abroad. Or perhaps you weren't looking for the Torrances. *(She moves to the divan and replaces the packet in her bag.)* Well, that's my chore done for the day, and I'm going. Good-bye, Sandra.

SANDRA. *(crossing to the divan for her wrap)* I'll come with you. No point in my staying, obviously.

JENNIFER. But what about John? He'll be coming.

SANDRA. Oh, John – well, he can…

(The buzzer sounds.)

JENNIFER. I expect that's him now. *(She crosses to open the door right, standing behind it.)*

*(**DAVID FORRESTER** enters right. He is a good-looking man of about thirty-eight. Behind his charm and manner, you sense a certain hardness and ruthlessness. An ambitious man. On seeing the two women he looks taken aback, but quickly masks his surprise. **SANDRA** on the other hand, displays real astonishment.)*

DAVID. Hullo, Sandra.

SANDRA. David!

JENNIFER. *(coming from behind the door)* Hullo!

DAVID. Hullo.

SANDRA. *(moving in to right of the divan)* Er – Mr Forrester – Mrs Brice.

JENNIFER. *(offering her hand)* How do you do?

DAVID. *(shaking her hand)* How do you do?

SANDRA. *(quickly)* You seem to have come on the wrong day, David – like me. Jennifer has just been telling me the Torrances are abroad.

DAVID. *(crossing to between the chairs)* Really. *(He smiles at **JENNIFER**.)* That seems to make three of us.

JENNIFER. *(indicating the cage)* Oh, I just came in to feed the budgerigar.

DAVID. *(vaguely; looking at the bird)* Oh, I see. Nice little fellow. *(He moves up to the cage.)* Does he talk?

JENNIFER. Only Swahili.

DAVID. Very expressive language, I've always understood.

JENNIFER. Well, I must fly. So nice to have seen you. *(She looks towards* **SANDRA** *maliciously.)* Good-bye, darling.

*(***JENNIFER*** exits right.* **DAVID** *crosses to above the coffee-table to put down his hat.)*

JENNIFER. *(re-enters)* Give my love to John, won't you? It's all been the greatest fun.

*(***JENNIFER*** exits right, closing the door.)*

DAVID. Who the devil was that?

SANDRA. Jennifer Brice.

DAVID. Friend of yours?

SANDRA. *(turning away towards the cabinet down left)* I wouldn't say so.

DAVID. What was she doing here?

SANDRA. *(stubbing out her cigarette in the ashtray on the cabinet)* You heard her. She came to feed the budgerigar. Whatever are you doing here?

DAVID. Darling – I came to see you.

SANDRA. *(turning to him)* Me?

DAVID. *(turning up stage)* By the way, whose flat are we in?

SANDRA. The Torrances'.

DAVID. *(enlightened)* Oh, I see. *(He looks round.)* Well, it's very nice and suitable. *(He smiles and crosses to the divan.)* Do both the Torrances sleep on this? Surely not.

SANDRA. I think it opens into a double.

DAVID. That's kind of it. Sandra… *(He kisses her passionately.)*

SANDRA. *(responding)* David…

DAVID. It's been quite a while.

SANDRA. Too long!

*(***DAVID*** kisses her.)*

DAVID. All of a week!

SANDRA. No. Monday – at the theatre…

DAVID. *(embracing her)* That wasn't what I meant.

(They sit on the divan.)

Has it been long for you, too?

SANDRA. An age. I wish we didn't have to be so secretive.

DAVID. Well, we do.

SANDRA. All this plotting and planning. It's such a bore.

DAVID. *(suddenly disengaging himself)* It won't always be like this – but just for now... That woman – damned awkward her butting in like that. What does she think?

SANDRA. About us?

DAVID. Yes.

SANDRA. Well – I'm afraid...

DAVID. She'll go away and talk, eh? What damned bad luck. We've been so careful up to now.

SANDRA. I told her I was expecting John to pick me up here.

DAVID. Did she believe you?

SANDRA. *(dryly)* She might have done – if you hadn't walked in.

DAVID. *(rising)* As I said – damned bad luck. *(He crosses towards the balcony door.)* I must say you did a very good job of looking surprised.

SANDRA. But I was surprised.

DAVID. *(turning to her)* How could you be, when you'd asked me to come?

SANDRA. *I didn't ask you to come.*

DAVID. *(taking it in)* You didn't?

SANDRA. No.

DAVID. But I got a message.

SANDRA. *(rising)* What message?

DAVID. *(moving to right of centre chair)* Would I meet Mrs Grey at five hundred and thirteen Alberry Mansions at six-thirty – this *is* Alberry Mansions, isn't it?

SANDRA. Of course it is.

DAVID. Well, then?

SANDRA. *(crossing to the chair centre and sitting on the downstage arm of it)* David – there's something very queer about all this. The Torrances rang up and asked me to come here for drinks.

DAVID. Here we go again. Who are the Torrances?

SANDRA. Michael and Pat. Just come home from the Middle East or Africa or somewhere. United Nations, UNESCO – that sort of thing.

DAVID. (*turning up stage, looking at the pottery, etc.*) Obviously. All the right trappings. So – the Torrances rang you up and asked you for drinks – and you came. Obviously it's the wrong day. No signs of preparation for a party. (*struck by a sudden idea*) How did you get in?

SANDRA. I rang – and then I found the door wasn't locked. The catch on the Yale was down.

DAVID. (*crossing to the door and examining the lock*) So it is. That's peculiar.

SANDRA. It's very peculiar. And the most peculiar thing of all is that the Torrances went to the South of France last Saturday, so how on earth could Pat Torrance ring me up the day before yesterday?

DAVID. (*moving in to above the coffee-table*) She rang you up herself? It wasn't a message?

SANDRA. No, it was Pat – at least I thought it was.

DAVID. But now you're not so sure? Did you recognize her voice?

SANDRA. I don't know her awfully well. She said, "Pat Torrance speaking." It never occurred to me that it wasn't her.

DAVID. (*moving above her to left of the pouffe*) There's something behind all this that I don't understand.

SANDRA. I don't, either. And I don't like it.

DAVID. (*moving to left of her*) But what's the point of it all? Ringing you up, pretending to be Pat Torrence, getting you to come here, getting me to come here by sending me a message – supposedly from you. What does it all add up to?

SANDRA. I wonder… (*She breaks off.*)

DAVID. *(looking at her keenly)* You've got some idea about it. Come on, tell me.

SANDRA. *(slowly)* I wondered if – it might not be – John

DAVID. *(astonished)* John?

SANDRA. Sometimes I've thought – that he'd begun to suspect – about us.

DAVID. *(sharply)* You never told me.

SANDRA. I thought I was probably imagining it.

DAVID. *(thoughtfully; moving to the cabinet)* John…But how would he tie up with the Torrances? Could he have got this Torrance woman to ring you up and…

SANDRA. That's absurd. John hardly knows her.

DAVID. *(moving to below right of the divan)* He might have managed to borrow their flat, and then got someone or other to ring up and pretend to be Patricia Torrance…

SANDRA. But why? Why?

DAVID. My dear girl, use your head. To catch us in the act. *Inflagrante delicto.*

SANDRA. Oh, I see.

DAVID. *(moving up left)* Perhaps he's got a couple of bowler-hatted private detectives hiding in the bathroom.

(**DAVID** *exits up left.* **SANDRA** *rises.* **DAVID** *re-enters.*)

Couldn't even hide a bowler hat in there. *(He crosses above the chairs to down right.)* And this place is as bare as your hand. *(crossing below the coffee-table to below the divan)* Probably means to come here himself and surprise us in amorous play!

SANDRA. What a beastly – disgusting thing to do!

DAVID. *(amused)* No good taking such a high and moral tone, darling. After all, a husband is justified, I suppose, in being annoyed if he finds his wife has taken a lover. *(He sits on the divan.)* How long have you been married now?

SANDRA. *(crossing below the table to right of it)* Three years.

DAVID. And old John is still inclined to be on the jealous side, eh?

SANDRA. *(turning to* **DAVID***)* Of course he's jealous, you know that. But on the other hand he's frightfully simple. Anyone could deceive him, *(She moves below the chair right.)* I was quite sure he hadn't got a clue – until just lately.

DAVID. Well, I suppose some kind friend has been around and told him the good news, though I must say we've always been careful enough.

SANDRA. *(bitterly; sitting in the chair right)* Somebody always knows.

DAVID. Yes. *(He rises and moves to left of* **SANDRA***.)* Well, in that case I think the best thing to be done is for us to – beat a hasty retreat. We'll meet at the usual place tomorrow – but be sure you're not followed. We certainly can't risk anyone...Get your things.

*(**SANDRA** rises and crosses to below the divan. **DAVID** reaches for his hat on the table. The buzzer sounds.)*

SANDRA. *(in a low voice)* Who do you think...

DAVID. Ssh! *(He crosses to* **SANDRA***, putting his hat on the cabinet.)* If it's John and he doesn't hear anything he'll go away again.

(The buzzer sounds again.)

SANDRA. The door – it's open.

DAVID. I wish I'd put the damned catch down.

(He seats **SANDRA** *on the divan.)*

For God's sake try to relax. Here, have a cigarette. *(He offers her a cigarette from his case.)* Go on!

*(**SANDRA** takes a cigarette. **DAVID** lights it for her, takes and lights one for himself, exhales, moves to above the chair centre, turns to* **SANDRA** *and shrugs.)*

*(**ALEC** enters right. He is a young man of twenty-eight or nine, effeminate, very elegant, amusing, inclined to be*

*spiteful. He has a very artificial manner and is dressed
in the height of fashion – even wearing gloves.)*

DAVID. *(cont.)* Alec!

ALEC. Hullo, David. Hullo, Sandra. Darlings, how
devastating. We three seem to be much too early for
the party.

SANDRA. *(relieved, rising and moving to between the chairs,
right of* DAVID*)* There is a party, then? We were just
wondering.

ALEC. *(crossing below the coffee-table to below the divan)* Yes,
it doesn't look much like it, does it? No *canapés*, no
baked meats, no olives.

*(*SANDRA *sits on the chair right.)*

(turning) I suppose the party is here? The Torrances
aren't giving it somewhere else, are they?

DAVID. *(sitting in the chair centre)* Well – well – we wondered.

ALEC. How long have you two been here?

SANDRA. *(quickly)* Oh, I came about five minutes ago and
David has just arrived.

ALEC. Oh, I see. *(He puts his hat on the divan.)* You didn't
come together.

DAVID. No.

SANDRA. *(at the same moment)* No.

*(*ALEC *looks at them. There is a pause.)*

Pat rang you, did she?

ALEC. No, it was Michael, as a matter of fact. Of course, he
is rather a vague chap. I don't know him all that well.
He just said would I roll along here to drinks six-thirty
P.M. onwards. So here I am…

DAVID. All dressed up!

ALEC. Well, I've been to the garden party. My dear, the
people nowadays! *(He looks round and moves to the cabinet
down left.)* Anyway, I gathered this was to be quite a do.

DAVID. Did Michael say so?

ALEC. No – he just said "drinks" – *(He opens the cabinet.)* but there are ways of saying things. Well, there's something. I'm sure he'd want us to celebrate. *(He picks up an almost empty whisky bottle.)* Oh! *(He replaces it and picks up a gin bottle.)* Ah, gin! All right? There seems to be tonic.

SANDRA. Fine.

*(**ALEC** pours out three gin-and-tonics)*

DAVID. *(with decision; rising and moving to below the cabinet)* Well, it seems to be quite clear what's happened. The Torrances *are* giving a party, but they're giving it somewhere else and either they thought we knew where they were giving it or they forgot to say.

ALEC. It's rather queer, though, isn't it?

*(**DAVID** crosses to **SANDRA** with two glasses)*

I mean, that they should have forgotten to say so to all three of us.

*(**DAVID** checks, then goes on to give **SANDRA** her glass.)*

(turning to face them, holding his glass and the tonic bottle) Well – "absent friends" seems the right toast. To the Torrances!

DAVID. The Torrances!

*(They drink. **DAVID** crosses to the divan and sits on the right end of it.)*

SANDRA. *(with elaborate pretence)* Somebody – it was Jennifer Brice, as a matter of fact –

*(**ALEC** replaces the tonic bottle.)*

– said that the Torrances were abroad. I didn't believe her, but now I wonder…

ALEC. Jennifer Brice! *(He moves to left of **SANDRA**.)* Has she been here?

SANDRA. She came to feed the…

DAVID. Budgerigar.

(ALEC moves up to the cage, then to below the chest, then sits on the up stage arm of the chair centre.)

ALEC. *(happily)* My dears, how intriguing. Now wait a minute, let me work it all out. The Torrances have gone away. Somebody else – we don't know who – has asked us three to come here. *(He rises and turns to DAVID.)* But why? Exciting, isn't it? Quite like one of those mysteries in books, *(He kneels in the chair, facing DAVID.)* Perhaps they'll expect us to hunt round for a clue – you know, that'll send us on to the next place. Yes. *(He rises and moves downstage, looking out front, then to below the divan facing up stage.)* Really, what extraordinary things the Torrances have! *(He picks up a coffee-pot from the shelves above the divan.)* I suppose they brought this back with them from Baghdad. Oh, what a strange nose it's got.

SANDRA. Yes, cruel.

ALEC. Darling, that's very penetrating of you. *(He replaces the pot and moves to between the chairs.)* Yes, it is cruel. It's odd, isn't it, but this whole flat looks rather cruel to me. So bare and cold. These four walls that hold you in, and just the minimum of necessities to live in it, *(He crosses to right of DAVID.)* What a horrible place to be shut up in if you couldn't get out.

DAVID. It's a perfectly ordinary modern flat, Alec. Now don't start thinking up things.

ALEC. You're so hearty, David. You won't let me have any pleasant imaginings. *(He crosses to the chest.)* Now this, I believe, is what is known as a Damascus bride chest. Seems to have worm in it. *(He moves to the Kurdish knife on the wall right, and removes it from its sheath.)* Ough! Here's one of those bloodthirsty knives that you stab your wife with when she's been unfaithful. *(Crossing to DAVID with the knife.)* The inlay on the hilt's rather nice, isn't it, David? Well, go on. Take it. It won't bite you.

DAVID. *(taking the knife)* Yes, splendid. *(He returns it to ALEC.)*

ALEC. *(taking the knife)* You're so inartistic. *(He moves to* **SANDRA***, giving her the knife.)* Don't you think it's nice, Sandra?

SANDRA. *(taking it)* Beautiful. *(She hands it back to* **ALEC.***)*

ALEC. *(moving to the terrace with the knife)* Now, what's out here? *(He re-enters the room.)* Five floors up. What a drop. *(He looks at* **SANDRA***, then moves back off to the terrace again.)*
Might be a cliff in Cornwall. Perfect for suicide. Oh – I've dropped it! *(He re-enters the room.)* The knife – I've dropped it. Not on anyone's head, fortunately. Now I suppose I'll have to go down and pick it up. *(He moves to below the divan and picks up his hat.)* What a bore. While I'm there I'll see if I can find a porter.

SANDRA. I don't think there is one.

ALEC. Well, there's an office. There must be a manager or manageress. *(crossing straight to the door right)* I'll just pop in and find out if the Torrances are away and if they've let this flat to anyone.

DAVID. We might as well all go…

ALEC. *(from the other side of the door)* No. You stay here, Finish your drinks. Make yourself at home. I shan't be long.

*(***ALEC*** exits right, closing the door and locking it.)*

DAVID. *(loudly and angrily; moving to the coffee-table and putting his glass on it)* Of course that ass *would* turn up here. He's got the most malicious tongue in London.

SANDRA. D'you think he thought it odd, the two of us being here together? *(She puts her glass on the coffee-table.)*

DAVID. I bet he did. *(He moves up to behind the chair centre.)* He'll probably go around everywhere telling people that we've got the Torrances to lend us their flat to meet in while they're away.

SANDRA. *(rising to below the divan)* We'd better go.

DAVID. *(stopping her)* No, wait a minute. If we go off together it looks bad. *(He moves to right of the divan.)* Isn't Alec rather a friend of John's?

SANDRA. Oh, in a way. The person Alec was really devoted
to was my first husband, Barry. He was really terribly
upset when Barry died.

DAVID. When he went over that cliff in Cornwall?

SANDRA. Yes. *(amused)* With the fuss Alec made anyone
would think I'd *pushed* Barry over.

DAVID. *(lightly)* Did you?

SANDRA. What do you mean?

DAVID. *(surprised)* Nothing, *(He turns away to behind the chair
centre.)*

SANDRA. I jolly nearly went over myself. *(She shivers.)* It was
terrifying. The whole cliff subsided after a heavy rain.

DAVID. *(thoughtfully)* So Alec doesn't like you very much.

SANDRA. *(moving down left a little)* I don't think he likes any
women.

DAVID. But he particularly doesn't like you?

SANDRA. *(turning to DAVID)* What are you getting at?

DAVID. I just wondered – if it could be Alec who's behind
this whole thing. Getting us here, I mean.

SANDRA. But why should he?

DAVID. *(following out his thought)* Getting us to meet here,
and then passing the word to John to come and find
us together.

SANDRA. *(moving in towards him)* That's ridiculous. Anyway,
if Alec had done that, why should he come here
himself? That would ruin the whole point of the thing.

DAVID. Yes, yes, you're right. *(He takes the two glasses from the
coffee-table to the cabinet down left, then crosses to the door
right, taking his hat with him.)* At any rate, we might as
well get out of here now. We'll go and join friend Alec
down below.

SANDRA. I must say I'd like to know the explanation of all
this – it does seems so queer. *(She moves to the divan for
her wrap and bag.)* I can't really believe that...

(DAVID, at the door right, rattles the handle.)

DAVID. Hullo, this door's locked.

SANDRA. Oh, I expect the latch has slipped back in the Yale.

DAVID. *(turning the Yale lock handle)* No, no, it's not the Yale. You see, there's another lock below – a mortice lock. *That* seems to be locked.

SANDRA. *(moving to left of the coffee-table)* But it can't be. We got in quite easily and…

DAVID. *(backing downstage apace)* Somebody seems to have locked it from the outside.

SANDRA. Locked us in, do you mean?

DAVID. Yes.

SANDRA. *(moving to below right of the coffee-table)* But that'i absurd. We can… *(She stops.)* Who locked it?

DAVID. Alec.

SANDRA. Alec? Why should Alec lock us in? *(She moves to the door.)* All we have to do is bang or shout.

(DAVID stops her, seats her in the chair right, then drops his hat on the coffee-table and crosses to below the chair centre.)

DAVID. No, don't do that. Wait a minute – sit down. We've got to think this out first. There's something very odd going on. It may be Alec or it may be someone else. *Somebody* got us here, pretending to you to be the Torrances, and sending me a message apparently from *you. (He stands between the chair centre and the divan.)* Whoever it is got us here, and now we're locked up here, together.

SANDRA. But it's absurd. We've only got to shout.

DAVID. Oh, yes, shout. And then what happens? A scandal. Here we are, meeting in somebody else's flat while they're away, obviously a guilty assignation of some kind – and then some practical joker has locked us in.

SANDRA. Then the sooner we call his bluff the better. *(She rises and crosses to the door right.)* We'll make a hell of a row and pass it all off as a joke.

DAVID. *(his manner getting curt and unpleasant)* I tell you I can't *afford a.* scandal! *(He moves below the divan.)* It'll absolutely ruin my chances of getting that appointment. If John were to bring divorce proceedings now, it'd be the end.

SANDRA. What a selfish brute you are. *(She crosses between the table and the chairs to right of* **DAVID**.*)* You don't think of anyone but yourself. What about me? What about my reputation?

DAVID. You've never had much of one.

*(**SANDRA** slaps his face.)*

(rudely) Sit down.

*(**SANDRA** sits on the divan.)*

Let me think. *(He moves up to between the chairs.)* Yes. Somebody laid a trap for us and we're caught in it. We've got to think of the best way out.

SANDRA. You still think it was John. I don't believe it.

DAVID. *(moving above right chair towards the door right)* It's Alec I'm thinking of. Alec hates my guts – always has. *(He moves up to the chest.)* Suppose that Alec worked upon John and... *(He stops abruptly, standing by the Kuwait chest, looking down at the ground.)*

SANDRA. What is it?

DAVID. *(kneeling at the chest, touching something on the floor)* Sawdust. A little heap of sawdust. These holes – they're not worm-holes. They've been drilled – four little round holes. *(He gets up and moves to right of* **SANDRA**.*)* Air holes, so that somebody could breathe.

SANDRA. *(rising)* What do you mean?

DAVID. *(taking her and swinging himself to her left, down left)* Supposing Alec worked on John's suspicions – supposing he suggested that John should hide in the chest and that he, Alec, would arrange to get us here together.

SANDRA. You mean – you mean that John's hiding now in that chest? He is there now? That he's heard all we've been saying – that – that...

DAVID. I think it's possible – quite possible.

(**SANDRA** *looks at the chest, then at* **DAVID**. **DAVID** *moves up to the chest, opens the lid, looks inside, then closes the lid and moves to right of the chair right.*)

My God!

SANDRA. *(crossing to the chair centre)* What is it? What is it? *(She moves to the chest.)*

DAVID. Don't! Don't look inside!

SANDRA. *(moving towards* **DAVID***, to left of the chair right)* What is it?

DAVID. *(taking her and seating her in the chair right)* Come and sit down. Now, don't *scream*. Keep your voice down. *(moving below the coffee-table to h of the chair centre)* We've got to keep our heads over this.

SANDRA. Tell me...

DAVID. It's John. He's there, in that chest. And he's dead.

(There is a pause.)

SANDRA. Dead? John?

DAVID. He's been killed. Did you do it?

SANDRA. Me? What do you mean?

DAVID. You were here when I came – you sent me a message...

SANDRA. Why should I kill John in a strange flat and ask you to come here?

DAVID. So that I should be in it with you, my dear. You've hinted once or twice that you'd like to marry me – and you knew divorce doesn't suit my book.

SANDRA. Do you think I want to get us both hanged for murder?

DAVID. No, you thought we'd get away with it. This is somebody else's flat, isn't it? People who are away. Who was to know that you or I had been here? There's no porter downstairs, no-one saw us come in, we've no connection with this place.

SANDRA. I might just as well say that you killed him. *(She rises.)* You came here perhaps, met John, killed him, put him in that chest and then went away, watched for me to arrive, and came back.

DAVID. Oh, for God's sake don't talk such rot. *(He moves to below the right end of the divan.)* The trouble with you is that you're so damnably stupid.

SANDRA. *(furiously)* You're saying what you really think now, aren't you? None of your famous charm. You're a louse, that's what you are – a louse and a rat!

DAVID. What about you? How many men have you hopped into bed with, I should like to know?

SANDRA. You bastard! You filthy, rotten bastard! *(She moves below the coffee-table to right of it.)*

(The telephone rings. DAVID *backs below the divan. They look at the chest, then* SANDRA *looks at* DAVID.*)*

(in a shaking voice) Who – who do you think it is?

(They face the telephone.)

DAVID. I don't know.

SANDRA. Should we…

DAVID. I think – not.

SANDRA. It may be just Alec ringing up from downstairs.

*(*DAVID *goes to lift the receiver)*

No – don't.

*(*DAVID *stops)*

Don't.

DAVID. I can't think. I can't think. *(He sits on the divan. After a pause he rises to answer the telephone.)*

(The telephone stops. DAVID *wipes his forehead.)*

SANDRA. If that was Alec, he'll think it very odd, won't he?

DAVID. If that's Alec he'll probably come up and see. *(He pauses.)* I don't think it was Alec.

SANDRA. Who do you think it was?

DAVID. I don't know. *(He moves to right of the pouffe.)* I don't know.

(SANDRA sits on the pouffe, facing up stage.)

I've got to think – we've got to think clearly. Somebody got us here, somebody got John here. *(He moves above the chair centre to between the chairs.)* Somebody's locked us in from outside. *(He moves to the door right.)* Alec. It must be Alec. *(He goes to the chest, lifts the lid, closes it and goes on to the terrace.)*

SANDRA. *(rising and breaking slightly to left)* What are you doing?

(DAVID re-enters to above the chairs.)

DAVID. D'you remember that Kurdish knife that Alec dropped over the balcony? He said he was going downstairs to pick it up.

SANDRA. What about it?

DAVID. Well, he didn't pick it up. It's still down there.

SANDRA. I don't understand.

DAVID. John was stabbed – with that knife. *(He moves towards her.)* Don't you see? The pattern's getting pretty plain.

SANDRA. *(wildly)* I don't see. *(She sinks to the floor, leaning on the left side of the pouffn.)* I don't see anything. It's like a nightmare.

DAVID. *(above right of the pouffe)* There's only one person behind this. Alec. He told Jim that we two had arranged to meet here and he suggested that John should bore some air holes in that chest and hide inside it. *(He moves to above the chair centre.)* Then he stabbed John and left him there. He went away and watched for us to arrive, and then he came back. *(moving to right of centre chair)* He drew our attention to that knife. He had his gloves on the whole time, you remember, He gave it to me to hold, made me take it. Then you took it. Don't you understand? Our fingerprints are on that knife – and there isn't a damn thing we can do about it, Then he went away and locked the door, locking us in with a murdered man. Two people who've the best motives in the world for murdering him.

SANDRA. But that's crazy – crazy...

DAVID. Your fingerprints, and mine, on the knife – nobody else's. And there's not a damned thing we can do but wait for the police to arrive.

SANDRA. The police? *(She rises.)* Why should the police arrive?

DAVID. *(moving to above the pouffe)* Don't you see that logically that's bound to be the next thing that happens – the next stage in Alec's plan?

SANDRA. *(moving to below the divan, facing left)* Alec must be mad – mad. Why should he do this to us?

DAVID. You said he was devoted to your first husband, Barry, You've only got to take one look at Alec to see what kind of devotion that was.

SANDRA. Well? What's that got to do with John?

DAVID. *(moving to right of* **SANDRA***)* Did you push Barry over that cliff?

SANDRA. Of course I didn't. I told you I...

DAVID. *(turning* **SANDRA** *to face him, and forcing her to sit with him on the divan)* Listen, Sandra, I don't care a damn whether you pushed him over or not. But we've got to have this in the clear because we've got to know Alec's reason. Did you? You were in love with John then, weren't you, but he was a straight, simple type. Barry was a rich man, John was poor. Divorce wouldn't have suited you. You were out on that cliff together, you and Barry, and the landslide happened. You saw your chance and you pushed Barry over. *(shaking her by the shoulders)* Didn't you? Didn't you?

*(***SANDRA***, very vaguely, dumbly, finally nods her head.)*

(releasing her) And Alec knew!

SANDRA. He couldn't have known.

DAVID. Alec knew his people. (*He rises and moves to above the chairs.*) He not only suspected – he was sure. He bided his time. You married John, then you got tired of John and started an affair with me. Then Alec saw his chance. To punish, as he'd put it, John and you and me. (*He turns to* **SANDRA**.) Mad – of course he's mad. The question is, what are *we* going to do now?

SANDRA. (*rising and crossing below the table to the door right*) We've got to get out of here.

DAVID. Of course we've got to get out of here, but *how?*

SANDRA. We can beat on the door. We can shout.

DAVID. (*circling the chair right to above the chair centre*) What the hell good will that do us? Somebody will come and let us out, then they'll find the body and there we shall be. Hauled in for murder and a defence so fantastic no counsel would listen to it. My God, you even told that Brice woman you were *expecting* to meet John here.

SANDRA. (*moving to below the chair right*) But we'll say Alec was here – we'll explain...

DAVID. (*moving to below the divan*) Idiot! Alec will simply deny the whole thing. He had his gloves on every moment he was here. He'll deny ever having been near the place. Probably got a very pretty little alibi cooked up somewhere.

SANDRA. Somebody must have seen him come here...

DAVID. In a rabbit warren like this? I doubt it. (*moving to the kitchen door*) Some way out – there must be some way out.

(**DAVID** *exits up left.* **SANDRA** *moves up stage between the chairs, nearly coming into contact with the chest She reacts and breaks down left.* **DAVID** *re-enters.*)

Two damned square hygienic little boxes!

(**DAVID** *goes out on to the balcony,* **SANDRA** *moves up stage between the chairs, facing the balcony.* **DAVID** *re-enters.*)

SANDRA. Isn't there a fire-escape?

DAVID. In the corridor outside, I dare say. From here there's nothing but a sheer drop. *(He crosses to the door right.)* There must be some way – some way.

SANDRA. The telephone! We could ring someone up. We could say…

DAVID. *(crossing below the table to the cabinet)* Yes, yes! Why the hell didn't I think of that before? *(He stops.)* Who could we ring up? What could we say? *(He sits on the divan.)*

*(**SANDRA** sits on the chair right. They look at each other, then look away. The telephone rings. They look at it.)*

SANDRA. *(after a moment or two)* Answer it! For God's sake answer it. It can't be worse than this.

DAVID. Yes. Yes, I think you're right there. *(He rises, moves to the phone, picks it up and stands there listening for a moment. He adopts a rather different voice.)* Hullo? *(He puts his hand over the receiver and turns to **SANDRA**.)* It's Alec.

SANDRA. *(rising)* Alec?

*(**DAVID** holds the receiver, listening. A voice can be heard, but not what it says. Then he drops the receiver back on the hook.)*

What is it? *(She crosses to right of the divan.)* What did he say?

DAVID. He said we were caught like rats in a trap – like the rats we are. He said that in three or four minutes the police would be arriving.

SANDRA. *(with a faint scream)* Police! *(She backs up stage towards the balcony.)* Police! No, no. There must be some way out.

DAVID. *(moving up centre between the chairs)* There's only one way out – through that window and down.

SANDRA. Suicide? You're mad, They'll believe what we say – we'll explain…

DAVID. We'll be charged with murder. We'll be convicted.

SANDRA. No! *(She looks towards the door right and the fanlight.)* There must be some way out – there must. *(She goes to*

*the coffee-table, sweeps it clear, takes it to the door right and
stands on it, putting one hand through the fanlight.)*

DAVID. What are you trying to do, you little fool? Claw you
way out! Claw your way out!

SANDRA. *(coming off the table and backing downstage towards
the divan, facing* **DAVID***)* I didn't do it. I didn't kill John.
It's all your fault. Why did I ever meet you? Why didn't
you leave me alone?

DAVID. *(moving to right of* **SANDRA***, and circling to left of her)*
You bloody little bitch, you got me into this.

SANDRA. I hate the sight of you. I tell you I hate the sight of
you. You're cold and hard and cruel and selfish as sin.
You've never given a damn for anyone in the world
except yourself.

*(***DAVID*** forces her on to the divan, his hands at her
throat, There is a knocking at the door right.)*

VOICE. Open the door. It's the police.

(David straightens up.)

DAVID. Let them do it

*(***SANDRA*** rises and moves to between the chairs.)*

You got away with it the first time, didn't you? But you
won't get away with it this time.

(The knocking is repeated.)

VOICE. Come on – open up!

SANDRA. *(turning to face him)* I hate you.

DAVID. *(circling below the chairs and* **SANDRA** *to above the chairs
and towards the door up left)* Or perhaps it'll be fifteen
years in a prison cell. And how will you care for that?

*(***SANDRA*** sinks onto the chair right.)*

Fifteen years in a prison cell.

(The knocking is repeated.)

VOICE. We'll break the door down.

DAVID. *(backing towards the divan and below it)* Why should they come for me? It's you they should be coming for, not me. You killed Barry, not me. *(He stands by the cabinet, facing the door right.)* Why the hell should I get involved?

(A banging starts on the door – solid, steady, paced. SANDRA laughs hysterically, stopping as she senses the meaning of the bangs on the door.)

SANDRA. Rats in a trap, that's what we are. Rats in a trap.

(The lights dim to a black-out and the curtain falls.)

SET DESIGN

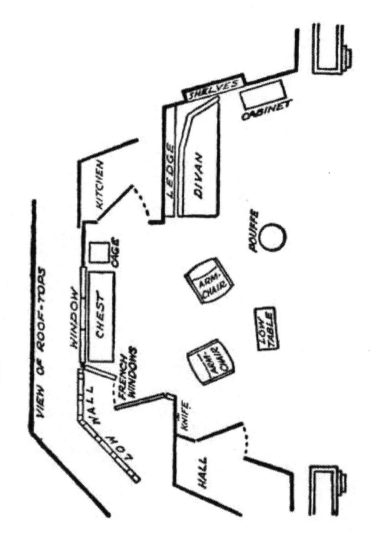

FURNITURE AND PROPERTY PLOT

Onstage: Cabinet (down left)

> *On it:* telephone, ashtray
>
> *In it: Top shelf:* 6 glasses, cocktail cherries
>
> *Bottom shelf:* bottle of whisky (almost empty), bottle of gin (half-full), a tonic splits, bottle-opener, matches,- corkscrew, soda-syphon

Shelves (above divan)

> *Top shelf:* empty
>
> *On 2nd shelf:* wooden head, illustrated vase
>
> *On 3rd shelf:* fertility god, Greek vase, Siamese lady
>
> *On 4th shelf:* two-headed vase, Roman vase
>
> *On 5th shelf:* camel head bowl, earthenware pot

Divan.

> *On it:* frill, mattress, 4 cushions
>
> *Over it:* tapestry
>
> *On shelf behind it:* 3 large coffee-pots, 1 small coffee-pot, 1 copper coffee-pot, a boxes, 1 bowl (ashtray) left end

Chest.

> *In it:* embroideries
>
> *Under it:* sawdust

Coffee-table.

> *On it:* ashtray, cigarette-box (empty)
>
> 2 empty chairs
>
> Pouffe
>
> Budgerigar cage
>
> > *On floor:* rugs
> >
> > *On wall right:* light fitting. Kurdish knife in scabbard. Mask
>
> Door up left, closed
>
> Door down *right*, closed, latch up, fanlight closed. Check key

Personal:

> **DAVID**: cigarette-case with 2 plain and 1 tipped cigarettes. Lighter
>
> **JENNIFER**: handbag with birdseed and key (Yale)
>
> **SANDRA**: handbag with cigarette-case and x tipped cigarette. Lighter
>
> **ALEC**: mortice key

LIGHTING PLOT

Property fittings required: 2 wall-brackets (dressing only)

Interior. A living-room

The Apparent Source of Light is a window up centre

The Main Acting Areas are centre, up centre, right centre and down left.

A fine summer's evening

To open: black-out

Cue 1   At rise of curtain

           Fade up to daylight

Cm 2   At end of Play

           Dim to black-out

EFFECTS PLOT

Cue 1   At rise of curtain

           Buzzer sounds – four short rings

Cue 2   A few moments later *Buzzer sounds –*

           one long ring

Cue 3   **SANDRA**: "John – well, he can…"

           Buzzer sounds

Cue 4   **DAVID**: "Get your things."

           Buzzer sounds

Cue 5   **DAVID**: "…he'll go away again."

           Buzzer sounds

Cue 6   **SANDRA**: "…filthy, rotten bastard."

           Telephone rings

Cue 7   **DAVID** rises from divan

           Telephone stops

Cue 8   **DAVID** and **SANDRA** look away from each other

           Telephone rings

Cue 9   **DAVID** lifts receiver

           Telephone stops

Cue io   **SANDRA**: "…except yourself."

           Knocking on door

Cue 11   **DAVID**: "…with it this time."

           Knocking repeated

Cue 12   **DAVID**: "…in a prison cell."

           Knocking repeated

Cue 13   **DAVID**: "…I get involved?"

           Solid, steady bangs on door right

The Patient

THE PATIENT was first presented by Peter Saunders at the Duchess Theatre, London, on December 29th, 1962. The Director was Hubert Gregg, with sets by Peter Rice. The cast was as follows:

LANSEN. . . . . *Raymond Bowers*

NURSE . . . . *Mercy Haystead*

DR GINSBERG . . . . *Robert Raglan*

INSPECTOR CRAY . . . . *David Langhn*

BRYAN WINGFIELD . . . . *Michael Beint*

EMMELINE ROSS . . . . *Vera Cook*

WILLIAM ROSS. . . . . *Robin May*

BRENDA JACKSON. . . . . *Betty McDowall*

THE PATIENT. . . . . *Rosemary Martin*

CHARACTERS

LANSEN

NURSE

DR GINSBERG

INSPECTOR CRAY

BRYAN WINGFIELD

EMMELINE ROSS

WILLIAM ROSS

BRENDA JACKSON*l*

THE PATIENT*n*

SETTING

A private room in a nursing home.

(Scene: A private room in a nursing-home. An Autumn afternoon. The room is square, plain and hygienic-looking. In the right wall are two sets of double doors. Across the back is a large window covered by Venetian blinds which are at present down but not "closed." Up left, and extending across half the wmdow is a curtained alcove, the curtains drawn back. Inside the alcove left is a cabinet. An electrical apparatus, with dials, red light, etc., is down left centre. A hospital trolley is up right centre in the window, and a wall telephone down right. Down right centre is a small table, with an elbow chair to right of it and four small chairs in a rough semicircle to left of it. These have the appearance of having been brought into the room for a purpose and not really belonging to it. On the trolley is a sterilizer with boiling water.)

(When the curtain rises, the lights fade up from a black-out. **LANSEN**, *a tall gangling* **YOUNG MAN** *with spectacles, wearing a long white hospital overall, is fiddling with an electrical apparatus on castors left centre. The* **NURSE**, *a tall, good-looking woman, competent and correct, slightly inhuman and completely submissive to everything the doctor says, is at the trolley up right centre. She lifts the lid of the sterilizer, removes a needle with a forceps, places it in a tray, crosses to the cabinet up left, takes out a towel, and crosses back to put it on the trolley. A buzzer sounds.)*

*(***DR GINSBERG** *enters up right and goes to the telephone down right. He is a dark, clever-looking man in his middle forties.)*

GINSBERG. All right, Nurse, I'll answer it. *(at the telephone)* Yes?... Oh, Inspector Cray, good. Ask him ta come up to Room Fourteen, will you? *(He crosses to right of the*

electrical apparatus.) How are you doing, Lansen? Got
it fixed up?

LANSEN. Yes, everything's in order. I'll plug in here, Dr
Ginsberg. *(He indicates a plug down left.)*

GINSBERG. You're quite sure about this, now? We can't
afford to have a slip up.

LANSEN. Quite sure, Doctor. It'll work a treat.

GINSBERG. Good. *(He turns and looks at the chairs.)* Oh, a
little less formal, I think, Nurse. Let's move these
chairs a bit. *(He moves the one which is third from left of
the desk, to the corner up right.)* Er – that one over there
against the wall.

*(**GINSBERG** exits by the doors down right.)*

NURSE. Yes, Doctor. *(She comes down and lifts the chair which
is left of the table.)*

LANSEN. Careful! *(He takes it and places it down left against
the wall.)*

NURSE. *(indicating the apparatus, with slight curiosity)* What is
this thing?

LANSEN. *(grinning)* New electrical gadget.

NURSE. *(bored)* Oh, one of those. *(She moves up to the trolley.)*

LANSEN. Trouble with you people is you've no respect for
science.

*(**INSPECTOR CRAY** enters down right and crosses to
right of the electrical apparatus. He is a middle-aged
man of delusively mild appearance.)*

*(**GINSBERG** enters with him and moves to behind the
table.)*

INSPECTOR. Good afternoon.

GINSBERG. Everything's ready.

INSPECTOR. *(indicating the electrical apparatus)* Is this the
contraption?

LANSEN. Good afternoon, Inspector.

GINSBERG. Yes. It's been well tested, Inspector.

LANSEN. It works perfectly. The least touch will make a connection. I guarantee there will be no hitch.

GINSBERG. All right, Lansen. We'll call you when we need you.

(*LANSEN crosses and exits down right.*)

(to NURSE) Has Nurse Cartwright got the patient ready?

NURSE. (*coming a step downstage*) Yes, Doctor. Quite ready.

GINSBERG. (*to the INSPECTOR*) Nurse Bond here is going to stay and assist me during the experiment

INSPECTOR. Oh, good. That's very kind of you.

NURSE. Not at all, Inspector. I'll do anything I can to help. I'd never have gone off duty, if I'd thought that Mrs Wingfield was unduly depressed.

GINSBERG. Nobody's blaming you, Nurse.

(*The NURSE moves to the trolley.*)

You say the others have arrived?

INSPECTOR. Yes, they're downstairs.

GINSBERG. (*moving below the desk to right of it*) All four of them?

INSPECTOR. All four of them. Bryan Wingfield, Emmeline Ross, William Ross and Brenda Jackson. They can't leave I've posted my men.

GINSBERG. (*formally*) You must understand, Inspector, that the well-being of my patient comes before anything else. At the first sign of collapse or undue excitement – any indication that the experiment is having an adverse effect – I shall stop the proceedings. (*to NURSE*) You understand that, Nurse?

NURSE. Yes, Doctor.

INSPECTOR. Quite so, quite so – I shouldn't expect anything else. (*uneasily*) You don't think it's too risky?

GINSBERG. (*moving right and sitting in the elbow chair; coldly*) If I thought it was too risky I should not permit the experiment. Mrs Wingfield's condition is mainly psychological – the result of severe shock. Her temperature, heart and pulse are now normal. *(to the* **NURSE***)* Nurse, you are already acquainted with the family. Go down to the waiting-room and bring them up here. If they ask you any questions, please be strictly non-committal in your answers.

NURSE. Yes, Doctor.

(The **NURSE** *exits down right.)*

INSPECTOR. *(moving and sitting left of the table)* Well, here we go.

GINSBERG. Yes.

INSPECTOR. Let's hope we have luck. Have any of them been allowed to see her?

GINSBERG. Her husband, naturally. And also her brother and sister for a few minutes. The nurse assigned to look after her here, Nurse Cartwright, was present all the time. *(He pauses.)* Miss Jackson has not visited Mrs Wingfield, nor asked to do so.

INSPECTOR. *(rising and crossing to above left of the chair centre)* Quite so. You'll give them a little preliminary talk, will you? Put them in the picture.

GINSBERG. Certainly, if you wish.

(The **INSPECTOR** *strolls up to the window.)*

I see that Mrs Wingfield fell from the second-storey balcony.

INSPECTOR. Yes. Yes, she did.

GINSBERG. *(rising and moving to centre)* Remarkable, really, that she wasn't killed. Head contusions, dislocated shoulder and fracture of the left leg.

(The **NURSE** *opens the door down right. The* **INSPECTOR** *moves to left centre.* **BRYAN WINGFIELD**, **WILLIAM ROSS** *and* **EMMELINE ROSS** *enter down right.* **WINGFIELD** *is a short, stocky man of about thirty-five, attractive, with a quiet manner normally and rather a poker face.* **ROSS** *is a man of the same age, also short, but dark-haired, rather mercurial in temperament.* **EMMELINE**, *his sister,*

is a tall, grim-faced woman of forty. They are all in a state of emotional disturbance. **NURSE** *exits down right.)*

(shaking hands with **EMMELINE**) Good afternoon, Miss Ross, will you sit down? *(He shakes hands with* **ROSS**.) Mr Ross!

(ROSS moves up stage right, near the door.)

Good afternoon. Mr Wingfield. *(He shakes hands with* **WINGFIELD**.)

WINGFIELD. You sent for us – it's not – my wife? There's not bad news?

GINSBERG. No, Mr Wingfield. No bad news. *(He passes* **WINGFIELD** *to his left.)*

(WINGFIELD moves above left of the chair centre.)

WINGFIELD. Thank God. When you sent for us I thought there might be a change for the worse.

GINSBERG. There is no change of any kind – neither for the worse, nor – alas – for the better.

EMMELINE. *(moving below the chair left of the table)* Is my sister *still* unconscious?

GINSBERG. She is still completely paralysed. She cannot move or speak.

EMMELINE. *(sitting left of the table)* It's terrible. Simply terrible!

INSPECTOR. Was Miss Jackson with you?

WINGFIELD. She was following us.

(GINSBERG moves to the downstage doors. **BRENDA JACKSON** *enters down right and crosses to his left. She is a tall, extremely pretty young woman of twenty-five.)*

Dr Ginsberg, my secretary, Miss Jackson.

GINSBERG. Good afternoon.

(BRENDA crosses left, below the chair centre, which **WINGFIELD** *indicates to her, below the electrical apparatus ti the chair down left. She turns and looks at the electrical apparatus.)*

ROSS. Poor Jenny, what an awful thing to happen to anyone. Sometimes I feel it would have been better if she'd been killed outright by the fall.

WINGFIELD. *(moving to left centre)* No. Anything but that.

ROSS. I know what you feel, Bryan. But this – I mean, it's a living death, isn't it, Doctor?

GINSBERG. There's still some hope for your sister, Mr Ross.

BRENDA. But she won't stay like this? I mean – she'll get better, won't she?

GINSBERG. *(crossing to right of BRENDA)* In cases of this kind – it is very difficult to forecast the progress of a patient. Her injuries will heal, yes. The bones will knit, the dislocation has already been reduced, the wounds in the head are nearly healed.

WINGFIELD. *(moving downstage to right of GINSBERG)* Then why shouldn't she get well? Why shouldn't she be herself again in every way?

GINSBERG. *(crossing below WINGFIELD to left of ROSS)* You are touching there on a field in which we are still ignorant. Mrs Wingfield's state of paralysis is due to shock.

EMMELINE. The result of her accident?

GINSBERG. Her accident was the ostensible cause.

ROSS. Just what do you mean by ostensible?

GINSBERG. *(crossing to right of the table)* Mrs Wingfield must have suffered unusual fears as she fell from the balcony. It is not so much her *physical* injuries but something in her *mind* that has produced this state of complete paralysis.

(**BRENDA** *sits in the chair down left.*)

WINGFIELD. *(moving above chair centre)* You're not trying to say –

(**GINSBERG** *sits behind the table.*)

– you're not thinking what I'm sure the Inspector has been more or less suggesting – that my wife tried to commit suicide? That I don't believe for a moment.

INSPECTOR. I haven't *said* I thought it was suicide, Mr Wingfield.

WINGFIELD. *(sitting in the chair centre)* You must think something of the kind or you and your people wouldn't keep hanging round like vultures.

INSPECTOR. We have to be quite clear as to the cause of this – accident.

ROSS. *(moving downstage level with the* **INSPECTOR**, *left of* **WINGFIELD***)* My God, isn't it simple enough? She's been ill for months. She'd been feeling weak, up for the first time, or practically the first time. Goes over to the window, out on to the balcony – leans over, is suddenly taken giddy and falls to the ground. That balcony's very low.

EMMELINE. Don't get so excited, William, don't shout.

ROSS. *(turning to* **EMMELINE***)* It's all very well, Bunny, but it makes me mad, all this business. *(to* **GINSBERG***)* Do you think it's pleasant for us having the police mixing themselves up in our family affairs?

WINGFIELD. Now, Bill, if anyone should complain it's myself, and I don't.

*(***ROSS*** moves up stage to the window.)*

BRENDA. What have we been asked to come here for?

INSPECTOR. *(moving above the table)* One moment, Miss Jackson. *(to* **EMMELINE***)* Miss Ross, I wish you could tell me a little more about your sister. Was she at all subject to fits of melancholy – depression?

EMMELINE. She was always highly strung, nervous.

ROSS. *(sitting in the chair up stage)* Oh, I wouldn't say that at all.

EMMELINE. Men don't realize these things. I know what I'm talking about. I think it is quite possible, Inspector, that her illness had left her particularly low and depressed, and that with other things she had to worry and distress her…

(**BRENDA** *rises and moves towards the door down right.*
The **INSPECTOR** *moves to right of her.* **GINSBERG** *and*
WINGFIELD *rise.*)

INSPECTOR. Where are you going, Miss Jackson?

BRENDA. I'm leaving. I'm not one of the family, I'm only
Mr Wingfield's secretary. I don't see the point of all
this. I was asked to come with the others, but if all
you're going to do is to go over and over again about
the accident – whether it was accident or attempted
suicide – well, I don't see why I should stay.

INSPECTOR. But it's not going to be the same thing over
and over again, Miss Jackson. We are about to make an
experiment.

BRENDA. *(arrested at the door)* An experiment? What kind of
experiment?

INSPECTOR. Dr Ginsberg will explain. Sit down, Miss
Jackson.

(**BRENDA** *moves back to her chair and sits.* **WINGFIELD**
and **GINSBERG** *sit.*)

Dr Ginsberg!

GINSBERG. I had better perhaps recapitulate what I know
or have been told. Mrs Wingfield has been suffering
in the last two months from an illness somewhat
mysterious in nature which was puzzling the doctor in
attendance on her, Dr Horsefield. This I have on the
authority of Dr Horsefield himself.

(The **INSPECTOR** *moves to above the table.)*

She was, however, showing decided signs of
improvement and was convalescent, though there
was still a nurse in the house. On the day in question,
exactly ten days ago, Mrs Wingfield got up from bed
after lunch and was settled by Nurse Bond in an easy
chair near the open window, it being a fine, mild
afternoon. She had books beside her, and a small
radio. After seeing her patient had all she needed,
nurse went out for her afternoon walk as usual. What

happened during the course of the afternoon is a matter of conjecture.

(The INSPECTOR moves to above left of WINGFIELD.)

But at half past three a cry was heard. Miss Ross, who was sitting in the room below, saw a falling body cross the window. It was the body of Mrs Wingfield, who had fallen from the balcony of her room. There was no-one with her at the time when she fell, but there were *four* people in the house, the four people who are assembled here now.

INSPECTOR. Perhaps, Mr Wingfield, you would like to tell us in your own words just what happened then? .

WINGFIELD. I should have thought I'd told it often enough already. I was correcting proofs in my study. I heard a scream, a noise from outside. I rushed to the side door, went out on the terrace and found – and found poor Jenny. *(He rises and moves to above the table.)* Emmeline joined me a moment later, and then William and Miss Jackson. We telephoned for the doctor and... *(His voice breaks.)*

GINSBERG. I – I...

INSPECTOR. Yes, yes, Mr Wingfield, there's no need to go into any more. *(He turns to BRENDA.)* Miss Jackson, will you tell us again your side of the story?

BRENDA. I had been asked to look up a reference in the encyclopaedia for Mr Wingfield. I was in the library when I heard a commotion and people running. I dropped the book and came out and joined them on the terrace.

INSPECTOR. *(turning to ROSS)* Mr Ross?

ROSS. What? Oh – *(moving down to the INSPECTOR, right of the chair centre)* I'd been playing golf all the morning – always play golf on a Saturday. I'd come in, eaten a hearty lunch and was feeling whacked. I lay down on my bed upstairs.

It was Jenny's scream that woke me up. I thought for a moment I must have been dreaming. Then I heard the row down below and I looked out of my window. There she was on the terrace with the others gathered round. *(fiercely, facing the* **INSPECTOR***)* Oh, God, have we got to go over this again and again?

INSPECTOR. I only wanted to stress the point that nobody who was in the house can tell us exactly what happened that afternoon. *(He pauses.)* Nobody, that is, except Mrs Wingfield herself.

ROSS. It's all perfectly simple, as I've said all along. Poor Jenny thought she was stronger than she was. She went out on the balcony, leant over, and that's that. *(He sits on the chair centre, takes off his spectacles and wipes them.)* Perfectly simple accident – might have happened to anybody.

WINGFIELD. Somebody ought to have been with her. *(He moves up to the window.)* I blame myself for leaving her alone.

EMMELINE. But she was supposed to rest in the afternoon, Bryan, that was part of the doctor's orders. We were all going to join her at half past four for tea, but she was supposed to rest every afternoon from three o'clock until then.

INSPECTOR. Miss Ross – *(moving above the chairs to above the table)* the accident seems a little difficult to explain. The railings of the balcony did not give way.

ROSS. No, no. She got giddy and overbalanced. I leant over myself to test it afterwards and it could easily happen.

INSPECTOR. Mrs Wingfield is a very small woman. It wouldn't be so easy for her to overbalance even if she was taken giddy.

EMMELINE. I hate to say it, but I think you're right in what you suspect. I think poor Jenny was worried and troubled in her mind. I think a fit of depression came over her...

WINGFIELD. *(moving downstage to above* **EMMELINE***)* You keep saying she tried to commit suicide. I don't believe it. I won't believe it.

EMMELINE. *(with meaning)* She had plenty to make her depressed.

WINGFIELD. What do you mean by that?

EMMELINE. *(rising)* I think you know quite well what I mean. *(She crosses below the chairs to right of* **BRENDA**.*)* I'm not blind, Bryan.

WINGFIELD. Jenny wasn't depressed. She'd nothing to be depressed about. You've got an evil mind, Emmeline, and you just imagine things.

ROSS. Leave my sister alone.

BRENDA. *(rising and facing* **EMMELINE***)* It was an accident. Of course it was an accident. Miss Ross is just trying to – trying to...

EMMELINE. *(facing* **BRENDA***)* Yes, what am I trying to do?

BRENDA. It's women like you that write anonymous letters – poison pen letters. Just because no man has ever looked at you...

EMMELINE. How dare you!

ROSS. *(rising and moving to up right)* Oh, my God! Women! Cut it out, both of you.

WINGFIELD. *(moving to down centre)* I think we're all rather over-excited, you know. We're talking about things that are quite beside the point. What we really want to get at is, what was Jenny's state of mind on the day she fell? Well, I'm her husband, I know her pretty well, and I don't think for a moment she meant to commit suicide.

EMMELINE. Because you don't want to think so – you don't want to feel responsible!

WINGFIELD. Responsible? What do you mean by responsible?

EMMELINE. Driving her to do what she did!

(Characters speak simultenously.)

ROSS. What do you mean by that?

WINGFIELD. How dare you!

BRENDA. It's not true!

(End of simulatenous speech.)

GINSBERG. *(rising and moving to above the table)* Please – please!

*(***WINGFIELD** *turns up stage.)*

When I asked you to come here, it was not my object to provoke recriminations.

ROSS. *(angrily)* Wasn't it? I'm not so sure. *(He wheels round and looks suspiciously at the* **INSPECTOR**.*)*

GINSBERG. No, what I had in mind was to conduct an experiment.

BRENDA. *(crossing to left of* **GINSBERG***)* We've already been told that, but you still haven't told us what kind of experiment.

GINSBERG. As Inspector Cray said just now – only one person knows what happened that afternoon – Mrs Wingfield herself.

WINGFIELD. *(sighing)* And she can't tell us. Its too bad.

EMMELINE. She will when she's better.

GINSBERG. I don't think you quite appreciate the medical position, Miss Ross. *(He crosses to right of the electrical apparatus.)*

*(***BRENDA** *sits left of the table.)*

It may be months – it may even be years before Mrs Wingfield comes out of this state.

WINGFIELD. *(moving down to right of* **GINSBERG***)* Surely not.

GINSBERG. Yes, Mr Wingfield. I won't go into a lot of medical details, but there are people who have gone blind as a result of shock and have not recovered their sight for fifteen or twenty years. There have been those paralysed and unable to walk for the same periods of time. *(He moves above* **WINGFIELD** *to between the chairs left of the table and centre.)* Sometimes another shock precipitates recovery. But there's no fixed rule. *(to the* **INSPECTOR***)* Ring the bell, plecise.

(The **INSPECTOR** *crosses and rings the bell below the doors down right.)*

WINGFIELD. I don't quite understand what you are driving at, Doctor. *(He looks from* **GINSBERG** *to the* **INSPECTOR**.*)*

INSPECTOR. You're about to find out, Mr Wingfield.

GINSBERG. Miss Jackson…

*(***BRENDA** *rises.* **GINSBERG** *moves the chair left of the table close to it, lifting* **EMMELINE**'s *handbag, which he hands to her at centre.)*

EMMELINE. Thank you. *(She crosses to down left.)*

*(***GINSBERG** *takes the centre chair and places it between the two sets of doors, crosses to the window and closes up the Venetian blinds. The lights dim.* **GINSBERG** *switches on the up stage lights.)*

GINSBERG. Inspector, do you mind?

(The **INSPECTOR** *switches on the downstage lights.* **LANSEN** *opens the doors up right and pulls on the* **PATIENT** *on the trolley, the* **NURSE** *following. They place the trolley downstage, parallel to the footlights, with the* **PATIENT**'s *head to right. The* **PATIENT**'s *head is heavily bandaged so that nothing of the features show but the eyes and nose. She is quite motionless. Her eyes are open but she does not move. The* **NURSE** *stands about two feet from the* **PATIENT**'s *head.* **LANSEN** *moves the electrical apparatus round and nearer to the* **PATIENT**. **GINSBERG** *moves above centre of the trolley.)*

WINGFIELD. *(moving right above the trolley)* Jenny, darling!

*(***EMMELINE** *advances but does not speak.)*

BRENDA. *(moving to behind the chair left of the table)* What's going on? What are you trying to do?

*(***WINGFIELD** *faces* **GINSBERG** *up centre.)*

GINSBERG. Mrs Wingfield, as I have told you, is completely paralysed. She cannot move or speak.

*(***WINGFIELD** *turns up stage.)*

But we are all agreed that she knows what happened to
her on that day.

BRENDA. She's unconscious. She may be unconscious –
oh – for years, you said.

GINSBERG. I did not say *unconscious*. Mrs Wingfield cannot
move and cannot speak, but she *can* see and hear; and
I think it highly probable that her mind is as keen as
ever it was. She knows what happened. She would like
to communicate it to us, but unfortunately she can't
do so.

WINGFIELD. You think she can hear us? You think she does
know what we are saying to her, what we're feeling?

GINSBERG. I think she knows.

WINGFIELD. (*moving to the head of the* **PATIENT**) Jenny! Jenny,
darling! Can you hear me? It's been terrible for you, I
know, but everything's going to be all right.

GINSBERG. Lansen!

(**WINGFIELD** *moves upstage.*)

LANSEN. (*adjusting the electrical apparatus*) I'm ready, sir,
when you are.

GINSBERG. I said Mrs Wingfield could not communicate
with us, but it is possible that a way has been found.
Doctor Zalzbergen, who has been attending her, and
who is a specialist on this form of paralysis, became
aware of a very slight power of movement in the fingers
of the right hand. It is very slight – hardly noticeable.
She could not raise her arm or lift anything, but she
can very slighdy move the two fingers and thumb of
her right hand. Mr Lansen here has fixed up a certain
apparatus of an electrical nature.

(**ROSS** *moves above* **GINSBERG** *to above right of the*
PATIENT *'s head.*)

You see, there is a small rubber bulb. When that
bulb is pressed, a red light appears on the top of the
apparatus. The slightest pressure will operate it. If you
please, Lansen!

(**LANSEN** *presses the bulb twice. The red light on the apparatus goes up twice.*)

Nurse, uncover the patient's right arm.

(*The* **NURSE** *moves below the trolley, lays the* **PATIENT**'*s arm on the coverlet, then moves above the* **PATIENT** *to right of* **GINSBERG**.)

Lansen, between the thumb and two fingers. Gendy.

(**LANSEN** *places the bulb in the* **PATIENT**'*s right hand and crosses to the electrical apparatus.*)

Now I'm going to ask Mrs Wingfield some questions.

ROSS. Ask her questions? What do you mean? Questions about what?

GINSBERG. Questions about what happened on that Saturday afternoon.

ROSS. (*moving above the table to face the* **INSPECTOR** *down right.*) This *is your* doing!

GINSBERG. The experiment was suggested by Mr Lansen and myself.

WINGFIELD. (*moving to above the head of the* **PATIENT**) But you can't possibly put any reliance on what might be purely muscular spasms.

GINSBERG. I think we can soon find out whether Mrs Wingfield can answer questions or not.

WINGFIELD. I won't have it! It's dangerous for her. It'll set her recovery back. I won't allow this! I won't agree to it.

BRENDA. (*warningly*) Bryan! (*She turns up siege to face* **WINGFIELD**, *then senses the* **INSPECTOR** *watching her, crosses to the chair left of the table, and sits.*)

GINSBERG. Mrs Wingfield's health will be fully safeguarded, I assure you. Nurse!

(**WINGFIELD** *moves away to between the doors. The* **NURSE** *moves over and takes up her position by the* **PATIENT** *with her fingers on the* **PATIENT**'*s wrist.*)

(to the **NURSE***)* At the least sign of collapse, you know what to do.

NURSE. Yes, Doctor. *(She takes the* **PATIENT***'s pulse.)*

(The **INSPECTOR** *moves in to right of the* **NURSE***.)*

BRENDA. *(almost under her breath)* I don't like this – I don't like it.

EMMELINE. I'm sure you don't like it.

BRENDA. Do you?

EMMELINE. I think it might be interesting. *(She goes and sits on the chair down left)*

(Characters speak simultaneously.)

ROSS. I don't believe for a...

WINGFIELD. Inspector, I hope...

(End of simultaneous speech.)

INSPECTOR. Quiet, please! We must have absolute quiet. The doctor is about to begin.

*(***WINGFIELD** *sits on the chair between the doors.* **ROSS** *moves down right. There is a pause.)*

GINSBERG. Mrs Wingfield, you have had a very narrow escape from death and are now on the way to recovery. Your physical injuries are healing. We know that you are paralysed and that you cannot speak or move. What I want is this –

*(***WINGFIELD** *rises.)*

– if you understand what I am saying to you, try and move your fingers so that you press the bulb. Will you do so?

(There is a pause, then the **PATIENT***'s fingers move slightly and the red light comes on. There is a gasp from all the four people. The* **INSPECTOR** *is now closely watching, not the* **PATIENT** *but the four visitors-* **GINSBERG,** *on the other hand, is intent on the* **PATIENT***.* **LANSEN** *is intent on his apparatus, and beams with pleasure every time the light goes on.)*

You have heard and understood what we have been saying, Mrs Wingfield?

(one red light)

Thank you. Now what I propose is this: when the answer to a question is "yes" you press the bulb once; if the answer is "no" you will press it twice. Do you understand?

(one red light)

Now, Mrs Wingfield, what is the signal for "no?"

(two red lights in rapid succession)

I think, then, it must be clear to all of you that Mrs Wingfield can understand what I'm saying and can reply to my questions. I'm going back to the afternoon of Saturday the fourteenth. Have you a clear recollection of what happened that afternoon?

(one red light)

As far as possible, I will ask you questions that will save you too much fatigue. I am assuming, therefore, that you had lunch, got up, and that Nurse here settled you in a chair by the window. You were alone in your room with the window open and were supposed to rest until four-thirty. Am I correct?

(one red light)

Did you, in fact, sleep a little?

(one red light) And then you woke up...

(one red light) Went out on to the balcony?

(one red light) You leant over?

(one red light)

You lost your balance and fell?

(There is a pause. **LANSEN** *bends over to adjust the electrical apparatus.)*

Just a minute, Lansen! You fell?

(one red light) But you did not lose your balance.

(Two red lights. A gasp from everyone.) You were giddy — felt faint?

(two red lights)

WINGFIELD. Inspector, I...

INSPECTOR. Sssh!

(WINGFIELD *turns away.)*

GINSBERG. Mrs Wingfield, we have come to the point where you have to tell us what happened. I am going to say over the letters of the alphabet. When I come to the letter of the word you want, will you press the bulb. I'll begin. A, B, C, D, E, F, G, H, I, J, K, L, M, N, O, P.

(one red light)

You have given me the letter "P." I'm going to hazard a guess — I want you to tell me if I am right. Is the word in your mind "pushed?"

(one red light. There is a general sensation. **BRENDA** *shrinks away, her face in her hands.* **ROSS** *swears.* **EMMELINE** *is still.)*

BRENDA. No, it can't be true!

ROSS. What the hell!

WINGFIELD. This is iniquitous!

GINSBERG. Quiet, please. I cannot have the patient agitated. Mrs Wingfield, you obviously have more to tell us. I'm going to spell again. A, B, C, D, E, F, G, H, I, J, K, L, M.

(one red light)

M? The letter "M" is probably followed by a vowel. Which vowel, Mrs Wingfield? A, E, I, O, U.

(One red light. The **INSPECTOR** *moves to left of* **LANSEN** *above the electrical apparatus.)*

M-U?

(one red light)

Is the next letter "R?"

(One red light. The **INSPECTOR** *and* **GINSBERG** *exchange a look.)*

M-U-R-... Mrs Wingfield, are you trying to tell us that what happened that afternoon was not an accident; are you trying to tell us that it was attempted murder?

(One red light. There is an immediate reaction.)

(Characters speak simultaneously.)

BRYAN. It's incredible! Absolutely incredible. It's impossible, I tell you, impossible!

BRENDA. *(rising)* This is nonsense. Poor Jenny doesn't know what she's doing.

EMMELINE. It's not true. She doesn't know what she's saying.

ROSS. Murder! Murder! It can't be murder! D'you mean someone got in?

(End of simulatenous speech.)

GINSBERG. Please. Quiet, please!

EMMELINE. She doesn't know what she's saying.

INSPECTOR. I think she does.

GINSBERG. Mrs Wingfield, did some unknown person come in from outside and attack you?

(two red lights sharply) Was it someone in the house who pushed you? *(a pause, then one red light)*

WINGFIELD. My God!

(The red light flashes several times.)

NURSE. Doctor, her pulse is quickening.

INSPECTOR. *(crossing close to* **GINSBERG***)* Not much further. We must have the name.

GINSBERG. Mrs Wingfield, do you know who pushed you?

(one red light) I'm going to spell out the name. Do you understand?

(one red light) Good. A, B.

(one red light) B. Is that right?

(several red lights)

NURSE. Doctor! She's collapsed.

GINSBERG. It's no good. I daren't go on, Nurse!

*(The **NURSE** moves to the trolley up stage for the hypodermic and comes down to the **PATIENT**, handing the syringe to **GINSBERG**. **BRENDA** sits left of the table.)*

Thank you, Lansen. *(He breaks the ampule head, fills the syringe and injects it in the **PATIENT**'s arm.)*

*(**LANSEN** switches off the electrical apparatus, removes the bulb from the **PATIENT** and the plug from the wall. He wheels the electrical apparatus into the curtained recess, and exits down right. **ROSS** crosses above the table and **PATIENT** to down left and sits facing up stage. The **NURSE** returns the syringe to the trolley up stage. The **INSPECTOR** moves below the **PATIENT**, facing up stage.)*

Nurse, would you unplug the sterilizer?

NURSE. Yes, Doctor.

*(The **NURSE** unplugs the sterilizer. **GINSBERG** moves to left of the small trolley, and with the **NURSE** wheels it to the left wall.)*

WINGFIELD. Is she all right?

GINSBERG. The strain and excitement have been too much for her. She'll be all right. She must rest for a while. We should be able to resume in about half an hour.

WINGFIELD. I forbid you to go on with it. It's dangerous.

GINSBERG. I think you must allow me to be the best judge of that. We'll move Mrs Wingfield up nearer the window. She'll be all right there.

*(**GINSBERG** and the **NURSE** move the **PATIENT** up stage, with her head near the doors up right, the **NURSE** at the head.)*

EMMELINE. *(crossing below the table to right of it)* There's not much doubt is there, who she meant? "B." *(She looks at **WINGFIELD**.)* Not much doubt about that, is there, Bryan?

WINGFIELD. *(moving to above the table)* You always hated me, Emmeline. You always had it in for me. I tell you here and now, I didn't try to kill my wife.

EMMELINE. Do you deny that you were having an affair with that woman there? *(She points at* **BRENDA**.*)*

BRENDA. *(rising)* It's not true.

EMMELINE. Don't tell me that. You were head over ears in love with him.

BRENDA. *(moving up stage slightly and facing the others)* All right, then. I *was* in love with him. But that was all over ages ago. He didn't really care for me. *(She faces front.)* It's all over, I tell you. All *over!*

EMMELINE. In that case it seems odd you stayed on as his secretary.

BRENDA. I didn't want to go. I – oh, all right, then! *(passionately)* I still wanted to be near him. *(She sit's left of the table.)*

EMMELINE. And perhaps you thought that if Jenny were out of the way, you'd console him very nicely, and be Mrs Wingfield Number Two...

WINGFIELD. Emmeline, for heaven's sake!

EMMELINE. Perhaps it's "B" for Brenda.

BRENDA. You horrible woman! I hate you. It's not true.

ROSS. *(rising and crossing above the* **INSPECTOR** *to left of* **WINGFIELD**) Bryan – and Brenda. It seems to narrow it down to one of you two all right.

WINGFIELD. I wouldn't say that. It could be "B" for brother, couldn't it? Or Bill?

ROSS. She always called me William.

WINGFIELD. After all, who stands to gain by poor Jenny's death? Not me. It's you. You and Emmeline. It's you two who get her money.

GINSBERG. *(moving a pace downstage)* Please – please!

*(**WINGFIELD** breaks up stage.)*

I can't have all this argument. Nurse, will you take them down to the waiting-room.

NURSE. Yes, Doctor. *(She moves above* **ROSS**.*)*

ROSS. *(turning to* **GINSBERG***)* We can't stay cooped up in a little room with all of us slanging each other.

INSPECTOR. You can go where you please on the hospital premises, but none of you is actually to leave the place. *(sharply)* Is that understood?

BRYAN. All right.

ROSS. Yes.

EMMELINE. I have no wish to leave. My conscience is clear.

BRENDA. *(going up to her)* I think – *you* did it.

EMMELINE. *(sharply)* What do you mean?

BRENDA. You hate her – you've always hated her. And you get the money – you and your brother.

EMMELINE. My name does *not* begin with a "B," I'm thankful to say.

BRENDA. *(excitedly)* No – but it needn't. *(She turns to the* **INSPECTOR**.*)* Supposing that, after all, Mrs Wingfield *didn't* see who it was who pushed her off the balcony.

EMMELINE. She has told us that she did.

BRENDA. But supposing that she didn't. *(She rises and crosses to right of the* **INSPECTOR**.*)* Don't you see what a temptation it might be to her? She was jealous of me and Bryan – oh, yes, she knew about us – and she was jealous. And when that machine there – *(She gestures towards the electrical apparatus.)* gave her a chance to get back at us – at me – don't you see how tempting it was to say "Brenda pushed me…" It could have been like that, it could!

INSPECTOR. A little far-fetched.

BRENDA. No, it isn't! Not to a jealous woman. You don't know what women are like when they're jealous. And she'd been cooped up there in her room – thinking – suspecting – wondering if Bryan and I were still carrying on together. It isn't far-fetched, I tell you. It could easily be true. *(She looks at* **WINGFIELD**.*)*

WINGFIELD. *(thoughtfully)* It is quite possible, you know, Inspector.

BRENDA. *(to* **EMMELINE**, *crossing to centre)* And you *do* hate her.

EMMELINE. Me? My own sister?

BRENDA. I've seen you looking at her often. You were in love with Bryan – he was half engaged to you – and then Jenny came home from abroad and cut you out. *(She moves to left of the table, facing* **EMMELINE**.*)* Oh, she told me the whole story one day. You've never forgiven her. I think you've hated her ever since. I think that you came into her room that day, and you saw her leaning over the balcony, and it was too good a chance to be missed – you came up behind her and – *(with a gesture)* pushed her over...

EMMELINE. Inspector! Can't you stop this kind of thing?

INSPECTOR. I don't know that I want to, Miss Ross. I find it all very informative.

GINSBERG. I'm afraid I must insist on your leaving now. The patient must rest. We should be able to resume in twenty minutes. *(He moves to the up stage light switch and turns off part of the lights.)* Nurse will take you downstairs.

(The **NURSE** *opens the door down right.)*

NURSE. Yes, Doctor. *(She opens the door down right.)*

*(***ROSS, EMMELINE, WINGFIELD** *and* **BRENDA** *move to exit.)*

INSPECTOR. Miss Ross, would you mind waiting a moment?

(They pause, then **BRENDA** *exits, followed by* **ROSS,** *the* **NURSE** *and* **WINGFIELD**.*)*

EMMELINE. Well, what is it?

(The **INSPECTOR** *eases the chair left of the table a little farther to left.* **EMMELINE** *sits on it. The* **INSPECTOR** *moves to behind the table.)*

INSPECTOR. There are one or two questions I should like to put to you. I didn't want to embarrass your brother…

EMMELINE. *(interrupting sharply)* Embarrass William? You don't know him. He has no self-respect at all. Never ashamed to admit that he doesn't know where to turn for the next penny!

INSPECTOR. *(politely)* That's very interesting – but it was your brother-*in-law* that I thought might be embarrassed by the questions I am about to ask you.

(He sits on the left edge of the table. GINSBERG *moves down centre.)*

EMMELINE. *(a little taken aback)* Oh, Bryan. What do you want to know?

INSPECTOR. Miss Ross, you know the family very well. A person of your – intelligence – would not be deceived as to what went on in it. You know the lives of your sister and your brother-in-law, and what the relations were between them. It is reasonable that, up to now, you would say as little as you could. But now that you know what our suspicions are – and the way they have been confirmed only a minute or two ago – well, that alters matters, doesn't it?

EMMELINE. Yes, I suppose it does. *(She puts her bag on the floor of her chair.)* What do you want me to tell you?

INSPECTOR. *(rising and moving to right of the table)* This affair between Mr Wingfield and Miss Jackson, was it serious?

EMMELINE. Not on his part. His affairs never are.

INSPECTOR. *(moving above the table)* There actually *was* an affair?

EMMELINE. Of course. You heard her. She as good as admitted it.

INSPECTOR. You know it of your own knowledge?

EMMELINE. I could tell you various details to prove it, but I do not propose to do so. You will have to accept my word for it.

*(*GINSBERG *crosses to the foot of the* PATIENT.*)*

INSPECTOR. It started – when?

EMMELINE. Nearly a year ago.

INSPECTOR. And Mrs Wingfield found out about it?

EMMELINE. Yes.

INSPECTOR. And what was her attitude?

EMMELINE. She taxed Bryan with it.

INSPECTOR. (*sitting on the top edge of the table*) And he?

EMMELINE. He denied it, of course. Told her she was imagining things. You know what men are! Lie their way out of anything!

(*The* **INSPECTOR** *and* **GINSBERG** *exchange a look. The* **INSPECTOR** *moves round to behind the elbow chair.*)

She wanted him to send the girl away, but he wouldn't – said she was far too good a secretary to lose.

INSPECTOR. But Mrs Wingfield was very unhappy about it?

EMMELINE. Very.

INSPECTOR. Unhappy enough to want to take her own life?

EMMELINE. Not if she'd been well and strong. But her illness got her down.

(**GINSBERG** *crosses to centre, above and right of* **EMMELINE.**)

And she got all kinds of fancies.

GINSBERG. (*showing interest*) What kinds of fancies, Miss Ross?

EMMELINE. Just fancies.

INSPECTOR. Why was Mrs Wingfield left alone that afternoon?

EMMELINE. She preferred it. One of us always offered to sit with her, but she had her books and her radio. For some reason she preferred to be alone.

INSPECTOR. Whose idea was it to send the nurse off duty?

GINSBERG. In private nursing that's standard practice. She would have two hours off every afternoon.

INSPECTOR. *(moving below the table to left of* **EMMELINE***)* Miss Jackson has told us that "it was all over ages ago," referring to her affair with Mr Wingfield. Do you say that that was *not* so.

EMMELINE. I think they broke with each other for a while. Or possibly they were very careful. But at the time of the accident, it was on again all right. Oh, yes!

INSPECTOR. You seem very sure of that.

EMMELINE. I lived in the house, didn't I? *(She pauses.)* And I'll show you something. *(She reaches for her bag, takes out a piece of notepaper and hands it to the* **INSPECTOR***.)* I found it in the big Ming vase on the hall table. They used it as a postbox, it seems.

    *(***GINSBERG** *moves to right of the* **INSPECTOR***.)*

INSPECTOR. *(reading)* "Darling, we must be careful. I think she suspects. B." *(He looks at* **GINSBERG***.)*

EMMELINE. It's Bryan's writing all right. So, you see!

GINSBERG. *(moving above the* **INSPECTOR** *to centre)* Do you mind if I ask a question or two?

INSPECTOR. No, Doctor, please do. *(He moves to above the table, then on to right of the elbow chair.)*

GINSBERG. I'm interested in those "fancies" you mentioned, Miss Ross. You had some particular fancy in mind, I think.

EMMELINE. Just a sick woman's imaginings. She was ill, you see, and she felt she wasn't making the progress she should have done.

GINSBERG. And she thought there was a reason for that?

EMMELINE. She was – just upset.

INSPECTOR. *(leaning on the table and stressing his words)* She thought there was a reason for it.

EMMELINE. *(uneasily)* Well – yes.

GINSBERG. *(quietly)* She thought those two were poisoning her? That's it, isn't it?

    (There is a pause. The **INSPECTOR** *sits on the table.)*

EMMELINE. *(reluctantly)* Yes.

GINSBERG. She said so to you?

EMMELINE. Yes.

GINSBERG. And what did you say?

EMMELINE. I told her it was all nonsense of course.

GINSBERG. Did you take any steps yourself?

EMMELINE. I don't know what you mean.

GINSBERG. Did you discuss it with the doctor attending her? Take any samples of food?

EMMELINE. *(shocked)* Of course not. It was just a sick woman's fancy.

GINSBERG. Well, it happens, you know. Far more often than is known. The symptoms of arsenic poisoning, it's almost always arsenic, are practically indistinguishable from gastric disorders.

EMMELINE. Bryan couldn't – he just couldn't.

GINSBERG. It might have been the girl.

EMMELINE. Yes! Yes, I suppose so. *(She sighs.)* Well, we shall never know now.

GINSBERG. *(moving to below the **PATIENT**)* You're quite wrong there, Miss Ross. There are ways of telling. Traces of arsenic can be found in the hair, you know, and in the finger-nails…

EMMELINE. *(rising to left of her chair and facing up stage)* I can't believe it! I can't believe it of Bryan! *(turning to the **INSPECTOR** agitatedly)* Do you want me any longer, Inspector?

INSPECTOR. No, Miss Ross.

*(**EMMELINE** moves towards the table to take the paper, but the **INSPECTOR** rises right of the table and picks it up first.)*

I'll keep this. It's evidence.

EMMELINE. Yes, of course.

*(**EMMELINE** exits down right.)*

GINSBERG. *(above the table, rubbing his hands)* Well, we got something.

INSPECTOR. *(sitting in the elbow chair)* Yes. *(He locks at the piece of paper.)* From the Ming vase in the hall. Interesting.

GINSBERG. It's his writing?

INSPECTOR. Oh, yes, it's Bryan Wingfield's writing all right. You know, he was quite a one for the ladies. Bowled them over like ninepins. Unfortunately they always took him seriously.

GINSBERG. Doesn't strike me as the Casanova type. Writes all those historical novels. Very erudite.

INSPECTOR. There's quite a lot of dirt in history. Oh… *(He notices he is in **GINSBERG**'s chair, rises, and crosses below the table to left of the chair left of it.)*

GINSBERG. Thank you. *(He sits in the elbow chair.)* So it wasn't all over!

INSPECTOR. Get four people all het up and accusing each other, get an embittered and malicious woman on her own and invite her to spill the beans – it gives one some material to work on, doesn't it?

GINSBERG. In addition to what you had already. What did you have?

INSPECTOR. *(smiling)* Just some good solid facts. *(He sits left of the table.)* I went into the financial angle. Bryan Wing-field's a poor man, his wife's a rich woman. Her life's insured in favour of him – not for a very large sum, but it would enable him to marry again, if he wanted to. Her money came to her in trust. If she dies childless, it's divided between her brother and sister. The brother's a wastrel, always trying to get money out of his rich sister. According to Bryan, she told her brother she wasn't going to pay for him any more. *(Thoughtfully)* But I dare say she would have done – in the end.

GINSBERG. So which is it? B for Bryan? B for Brenda? B for Brother Bill? Or Emmeline without a B?

INSPECTOR. *(rising and moving centre)* Emmeline without the – Emmeline? Wait a minute – something I heard this afternoon, while they were all here... No, it's gone.

GINSBERG. Could it be B for burglar?

INSPECTOR. No, that's definitely out. We've got conclusive evidence on that point. The road was up in front of the house and there was a constable on duty there. Both the side and the front gate were directly under his eye. Nobody entered or left the house, that afternoon.

GINSBERG. You know, you asked me to co-operate, but you were very careful not to put all your cards on the table. Come on! What *do* you think?

INSPECTOR. It's not a question of thinking. *(He sits left of the table.)* I know.

GINSBERG. What?

INSPECTOR. I may be wrong, but I don't think so. You think it over.

*(**GINSBERG** enumerates on his fingers.)*

You've got seven minutes.

GINSBERG. Huh! Oh, yes. *(He rises and moves to above and right of the **PATIENT**.)*

*(The **INSPECTOR** rises and moves to left of the **PATIENT**.)*

Mrs Wingfield. Thank you for your help, Mrs. Wingfield. We come now to the crucial moment in the experiment.

INSPECTOR. Mrs Wingfield, we are about to leave you here, apparently unguarded. None of the suspects knows that you regained your powers of speech yesterday. They don't know that you did not in fact see who pushed you off that balcony. You realize what that means?

PATIENT. One of them will – will try to...

INSPECTOR. Someone will almost certainly enter this room.

GINSBERG. Are you sure you want to go through with this, Mrs Wingfield?

PATIENT. Yes, yes. I must know – I must know who…

INSPECTOR. Don't be afraid. We shall be close at hand. If anyone approaches you or touches you…

PATIENT. I know what to do.

INSPECTOR. Thank you, Mrs Wingfield, you're a wonderful woman. Just be brave for a few moments longer and we shall trap our killer. Trust me. Trust both of us, eh?

GINSBERG. Ready?

(They move the trolley downstage.)

INSPECTOR. Right.

GINSBERG. *(crossing to the downstage doors)* Why don't you come into my office? *(holding the door open)* In view of this poisoning suggestion, you might like to look over the files.

INSPECTOR. *(crossing to the downstage door)* Yes, I'd like another look at those X-ray plates too, if I may. *(He switches off the downstage lights.)*

*(***GINSBERG*** and the ***INSPECTOR*** exit down right. When off, they switch off the light in the passage. In the black-out, the ***NURSE*** enters up stage, with a small syringe, and crosses left to behind the curtain.)*

PATIENT. Help! Help!!

*(The ***INSPECTOR*** enters downstage.)*

INSPECTOR. All right, Mrs Wingfield, we're here!

*(***GINSBERG*** enters up stage and switches on the lights by the up stage switch. He rushes straight to above the ***PATIENT***.)*

PATIENT. Help! Murder! *(pointing to the curtains)* There!

*(The ***INSPECTOR*** crosses to left of the ***PATIENT***.)*

INSPECTOR. Is she all right?

GINSBERG. She's all right. You've been very brave, Mrs Wingfield.

INSPECTOR. Thank you, Mrs Wingfield. The killer has played right into our hands. *(He faces ***GINSBERG***.)*

That note in the Ming vase was all I needed. Bryan Wingfield would hardly need to write secret notes to a secretary he sees every day. He wrote that note to someone else. And that constable on duty. He swears that nobody entered or left the house that afternoon. *(He faces the curtain.)* So it seems you didn't take your off-duty walk that day. *(He moves to the left wall, facing onstage.)* You may come out from behind that curtain now, Nurse Bond.

(NURSE BOND *comes out from behind the curtain and takes a pace downstage. The lights black-out and – the curtain falls.)*

SET DESIGN

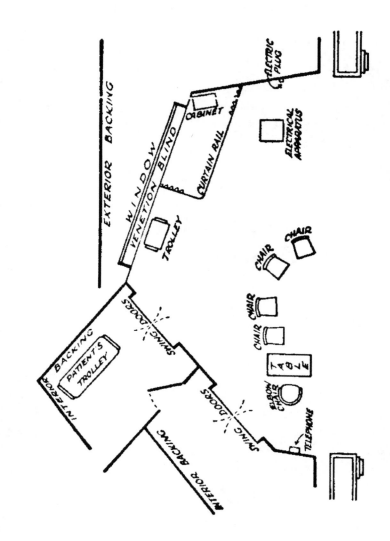

FURNITURE AND PROPERTY PLOT

Onstage: Electrical apparatus (left centre), unplugged

Cabinet (in cubicle up left)

In it: towel

Trolley

On top shelf: sterilizer (plugged to wall), kidney dish with hypodermic, bottle of injecticide, tray with forceps and instruments, dish with lint

On bottom shelf: bowl, cotton wool (2 packets)

Table

Elbow chair 4 small chairs

Above door up right: electric light switch

Below door down right: electric light switch, bell-push house wall, telephone

Cubicle up left, curtains open

Window, Venetian blinds down but "open"

Doors up right, closed

Doors down right, closed

Offstage: File (**DR GINSBERG**)

Trolley bed, mattress, sheets, pillows, cover (**PATIENT**)

Hypodermic (**NURSE**)

Black cape (**NURSE**)

Personal: Spectacles (**LANSEN**)

Screwdriver (**LANSEN**)

Spectacles (**DR GINSBERG**)

Watch with chain (**DR GINSBERG**)

Watch (**INSPECTOR**)

Handbag (**BRENDA**)

Handbag with note on scrap of paper (**EMMELINE**)

LIGHTING PLOT

Property fittings required: 1 hanging lamp up stage, 1 hanging lamp downstage

Interior. A nursing-home room

The Apparent Sources of Light are, in daylight, a window up centre; at night, 2 hanging lamps

The Main Acting Areas are right centre, down centre, left centre, down left, up right centre and up centre

To open: black-out

Cue 1   At rise of curtain

            Fade up to daylight Fittings off

Cue 2   **GINSBERG** closes the blinds

            Dim light to ¼

Cue 3   **GINSBERG** turns on lights up stage

            Snap in up stage lamp Snap in covering lights

Cue 4   **INSPECTOR** turns on lights downstage)

            Snap in downstage lamp Snap in covering lights

Cue 5   **GINSBERG** turns out up stage lights

            Snap out up stage lamp Snap out covering lights

Cue 6   **INSPECTOR** turns out downstage lights)

            black-out *onstage*

Cue 7   **INSPECTOR** and **GINSBERG** exit)

            Snap out lights in corridors

Cue 8   **GINSBERG** turns on up stage lights

            Snap in up stage lamp Snap in covering lights

Cue 9   At end of Play

            Quick fade to black-out

EFFECTS PLOT

Cue 1   **NURSE** puts towel on trolley
Telephone buzzer

Cue 2   **GINSBERG**: "If you please, Lansen."
Two red lights on apparatus

Cue 3   **GINSBERG**: "Will you do so?"
One red light

Cue 4   **GINSBERG**: "…saying, Mrs Wingfield?"
One red light

Cue 5   **GINSBERG**: "Do you understand?"
One red light

Cue 6   **GINSBERG**: "…signal for 'no'?"
Two red lights

Cue 7   **GINSBERG**: "…happened that afternoon."
One red light

Cue 8   **GINSBERG**: "Am I correct?"
One red light

Cue 9   **GINSBERG**: "…sleep a little?"
One red light

Cue 10   **GINSBERG**: "…you woke up."
One red light

Cue 11   **GINSBERG**: "…to the balcony?"
One red light

Cue 12   **GINSBERG**: "You leant over?"
One red light

Cue 13   **GINSBERG**: "…and fell?")
One red light

Cue 14   **GINSBERG**: "…not lose your balance."
Two red lights

Cue 15   **GINSBERG**: "…felt faint?")
Two red lights

Cue 16   **GINSBERG** : "…K, L, M, N, O, P."
One red light

Cue 17   **GINSBERG**: "…your mind 'pushed'?"
One red light

Cue 18   **GINSBERG**: "…J, K, L, M.")
One red light

EFFECTS PLOT

Cue 1 **NURSE** puts towel on trolley
     Telephone buzzer

Cue 2 **GINSBERG**: "If you please, Lansen."
     Two red lights on apparatus

Cue 3 **GINSBERG**: "Will you do so?"
     One red light

Cue 4 **GINSBERG**: "…saying, Mrs Wingfield?"
     One red light

Cue 5 **GINSBERG**: "Do you understand?"
     One red light

Cue 6 **GINSBERG**: "…signal for 'no'?"
     Two red lights

Cue 7 **GINSBERG**: "…happened that afternoon."
     One red light

Cue 8 **GINSBERG**: "Am I correct?"
     One red light

Cue 9 **GINSBERG**: "…sleep a little?"
     One red light

Cue 10 **GINSBERG**: "…you woke up."
     One red light

Cue 11 **GINSBERG**: "…to the balcony?"
     One red light

Cue 12 **GINSBERG**: "You leant over?"
     One red light

Cue 13 **GINSBERG**: "…and fell?")
     One red light

Cue 14 **GINSBERG**: "…not lose your balance."
     Two red lights

Cue 15 **GINSBERG**: "…felt faint?")
     Two red lights

Cue 16 **GINSBERG** : "…K, L, M, N, O, P."
     One red light

Cue 17 **GINSBERG**: "…your mind 'pushed'?"
     One red light

Cue 18 **GINSBERG**: "…J, K, L, M.")
     One red light

Cue 19   **GINSBERG**: "M?"
           One red light
Cue 20   **GINSBERG**: "A, E, I, O, U.")
           One red light
Cue 21   **GINSBERG**: "M, U?"
           One red light
Cue 22   **GINSBERG**: "…next letter 'R'?")
           One red light
Cue 23   **GINSBERG**: "…attempted murder?"
           One red light
Cue 24   **GINSBERG**: "…and attack you?")
           Two red lights sharply
Cue 25   **GINSBERG**: "…who pushed you?"
           Pause, then one red light
Cue 26   **WINGFIELD**: "My God!"
           Several red lights
Cue 27   **GINSBERG**: "…who pushed you?"
           One red light
Cm 28   **GINSBERG**: "Do you undentand?"
           One red light
Cue 29   **GINSBERG**: "A, B."
           One red light
Cue 30   **GINSBERG**: "B. Is that right?"
           Several red lights